LATTES AND SPIRITS

A Witch & Ghost Mystery

ALYN TROY

LATTES AND SPIRITS

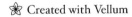

AUTHOR'S NOTE: WELSH NAMES

A note on Welsh Pronunciations and names:

Welsh is a Celtic Language, but one different from the Irish and Scottish versions. They do have very similar pronunciations with some key differences. Northern and Southern Welsh natives have differing accents as well.

Rather than add a guide here, I've tried to let April/Ebrel use her ears to show how Welsh words and names sound. I may not always get them correct. Any errors are on the part of my own American ears mishearing the videos I refer to online.

Ebrel is a Cornish variant of Ebrill, the Welsh name for April. I settled on this version because of how a double-L is pronounced in Welsh. The American version of English has no sound similar to it.

The author, who cannot even trill or roll their Rs (much to the chagrin of my Spanish teacher many years ago) has enough trouble pronouncing normal words. The author prefers not to mangle the beautiful sound of the Welsh language when pronouncing the main character's name, and settled on another British variant that sounds very similar to "April."

Welsh is a beautiful language, and there is a plethora of online resources. The author encourages you, dear reader, to explore the Welsh language on your own via YouTube, or Google.

In case you wonder... a W in the Welsh language is pronounced as a oo sound, as in Zoo. So, Pwca is Pookah.

The alarm clock blared. I popped open one eye.

4:30. I slapped the snooze. Then slapped it again because I had only drifted off about two hours ago. I hated jet lag.

"Ebrel, dearie!" Aunt Rose's voice kept me from pulling the pillow around my head and drifting back to sleep. Her Welsh accent and use of my British name pinged my brain enough to make me move. Guilt is a wonderful motivator. I couldn't let her down.

"I'm up!" I shouted and reached for the bedside light. Where was the switch? Probably one of those old-lady-on-the-cord ones. I'd never find it in the dark. Four hours ago, I had used the wall switch for the overhead.

I didn't think I could make it to the wall switch without great risk of breaking one or more of my toes by slamming them into one of the multitude of antique furniture and whatnots that Aunt Rose had crammed into this room.

Instead, I let my magic tingle through my fingers. I found the bulb inside the shade. The little magical ball of light I made could stay in there, hidden from sight. The lamp shade glowed. As long as Aunt Rose didn't turn it off, she wouldn't know I'd used magic. That was something I needed to keep secret.

Now that I could see, I grumbled and reached for my toiletries bag.

"I left a towel out for you, dearie," Rose called again. "Come on down when you can. I be dying to learn how to use this new foo-foo drink machine."

Ugh! First morning in the café. I was the only one who knew how to run the espresso machine. With jet lag and only two hours of sleep. Back in the States, I'd be heading to bed about now.

"Put on your big-girl-barista pants, April," I muttered and stumbled my way to the bath. Rose's flat above the café had the toilet in another room next to the bath. That was the "loo," she explained. The bath was where one bathed or washed up. Quaint. Living in Wales would take some getting used to.

The warmth of the shower felt so good I didn't want to leave it. Another week, and I might be over my jet lag. Until then, all I could do was work through it. I was committed. Misty Valley was my new home.

A moment later, dry and with the towel wrapped around me, I opened the door. Jake stood in the hallway. I sucked in a breath and tried to hold in my squeal of shock. No need to alarm Aunt Rose. It wasn't every girl who was haunted by the ghost of her dead boyfriend.

"Don't drop chicken feathers in my aunt's hallway," I whispered and slid into my room. I shut the door quickly and spun around. Jake floated there, still covered in chicken feathers. Even his leather jacket, the one he wore on when his bike swerved off the road, was coated in ghostly feathers.

"Happy Birthday, April," he said.

"Well, you're not about to see me in my birthday suit. I need to get dressed."

"I've seen it before," he said. "What's the big deal?"

"One, we're not dating anymore," I said. "Two, you're dead, and it's creepy."

"What's the problem?" Jake was so dense sometimes. "I just came to—"

A spark of magic leapt from my finger to the zipper on his jacket, and he winked out of sight.

"You too," I said and touched the ghostly chicken that materialised with him.

That would only give me a minute before he returned. Pesky ghost. And most girls thought living boyfriends could be annoying.

I had my yoga pants on and wiggled my arms and head through my long cable-knit sweater when I smelled wet feathers again.

"What did you do that for?"

"You wouldn't understand," I said when I popped my head through the sweater.

"I just wanted to hang out with you on your birthday," he said. This time two chickens popped in with him. One was pecking at dust under the bedside table. The other was perched on the curved wood of the headboard.

"I know, it's your death day too, and you don't want to be alone."

"The chickens aren't much company," he said and sat next to me on the bed.

"I wish you were useful while you're here. Pardon," I said and reached through his misty green form for my boots. "Look, I can't be shooing you away every few minutes. Today is very important. Don't screw it up for me."

"How would I do that?"

3

"First, don't ask me questions." I stood and poked a finger at his face. Jake flinched, probably afraid I'd spark him again. "The talking-to-myself excuse only works once a day."

The chicken on the headboard flapped and jumped onto Jake's shoulder.

"And take that feather," I said, pointing to my pillow.

"Sorry," he said. When his fingers touched the feather, it went ghostly again.

"Did you ever figure out why only a few ghost feathers turn solid again?"

He stuck it to the others on his leather jacket. "None of the other ghosts know. They guess that it's because I want to be with you. Some of that energy makes something small, like a feather, become real again. At least I can zap 'em back to the ghost realm when they do pop over."

"Keep an eye out for feathers," I said. "Aunt Rose will have a hissy fit if she thinks I brought a chicken in here."

"As allergic as you are to cats, I doubt she'd blame you for chickens."

"Yesterday was the first time I met her since I was five. She normally only called me on my birthday."

"Ebrel, dearie!" Rose's voice called from the café. "Are you coming down?"

"Don't get me in trouble!" I whispered in a hiss and poked Jake again.

Downstairs, Aunt Rose and our employee, Nia, waited behind the counter.

"The drink you made yesterday was magical," Nia said in her high voice. "Will you make me another?"

"Not yet." I waved them out of my way and grabbed my teal apron. Aunt Rose used the teal along with a pink in her decor and signage for Mystic Brews, the new name of her café. New, because I was here to be her partner and chief barista.

"Nia, be a dear and go check on the pastries I put in the oven," Aunt Rose said. Nia bobbed her head of dark wavy hair. She was way too full of bouncing energy for this early in the morning.

My aunt was everything I expected of an "Aunt Rose." A tad on the plump side. Ageing beauty lined her face, crinkled with laugh and smile lines. Her blue eyes matched mine, and a few strands of auburn streaked her grey hair. She would have cut a fine figure, as my father said, in her younger days. Now, she had that grandmotherly air about her, despite not having any children of her own.

Behind her apron, she wore a long-sleeved cardigan over a white blouse. The sweater had roses knitted on the collar and cuffs. She passed me a plate. "Have a scone, dearie. Once we get going, we won't be stopping. The whole village wants to meet you. I've got cream in the back if you want to spice it up."

"This is fine," I said, then turned and did a quick inventory. I nibbled on the scone while prepping. Pitchers, spoons in the ice bath, thermometers, porta-filters, the handled metal bowls where I packed the espresso grounds before the machine worked its high-pressured magic on them—all of it was there. And the pastry was divine. I remembered Mom saying her aunt's baking was the best ever. Anywhere. Full stop. She was correct. This was the best I ever tasted.

Aunt Rose answered a knock on the door.

"Red! Meet my niece Ebrel."

"Pleased ta meet the famed Ebrel, lassie," the man said. He held out a thick hand covered in curly red hair. He had a firm grip and calloused fingers.

"Red is Misty Valley's handyman, dearie," Aunt Rose said. "He's come to look at the ovens for me. We've got a hot spot I need to even out."

"Probably just be a faulty temperature probe," he said.

I washed my hands once he was back in the kitchen. Fortunately, there was a full, though small, pump jar of soap by the sink. I'd never been nailed with a health citation in my years as a barista, and I would not get one here. I glanced at the second grinder by the espresso machine. Then I checked the stock cupboard next to the sink. Regular beans, but no decaf espresso. "I forgot to grab the decaf beans. We do have them, right?"

"I think so. They should be in the cellar," Aunt Rose said. "I can send Nia."

"No worries, I can go check."

Down the stairs, the lights started to glow as I opened the door to the cellar. There was no light switch, and I didn't see magnetic sensors on the door frame. I'd have to check with Red and see how the place was wired. That was a good motion sensor if it caught me at the top of the stairs.

Even though the building was old, the damp, dusky odour I expected was absent. Instead, the aroma of coffee, flour, and all manner of food stuff wafted to me.

The coffee beans sat right where I had seen them yesterday. One row of bags extended out a few inches. I pushed them back, and the bags shook and hissed. I leapt back, magic surging into my hands.

An orange streak darted sideways from the shelf. A cat.

Huh. Aunt Rose said she didn't have any cats. Why was that one here? How did it get in?

I tried to hold my breath and not get any of the dander in my nose as I grabbed a bag of decaf beans, already roasted, and dashed up the stairs.

"There was a cat!" I set the beans on the counter next to Aunt Rose.

"Orange?"

I nodded, taking a few deep breaths.

"I'm sorry, dearie." She pulled a tissue from inside her left sleeve. I waved it off. So far, I was doing fine. Why did grand-motherly types always have tissues and whatnots up their sleeves?

"Thank you... Diolch," I said, remembering the Welsh word for thank you. "No need. I escaped without harm." No symptoms of being around a cat at all.

"Oh, that's good for you, dearie." She turned towards the kitchen. "Nia, Punkin got in again. Would you shoo him out? Ebrel is deathly allergic."

"We all be allergic to that furball," Red's voice drifted out. "You'll have a crowd in a jiffy ready to try Miss Ebrel's fancy new coffee. I'll see if I kin chase him off for a wee bit."

I glanced at the clock. Aunt Rose said we opened at six. Fifteen minutes from now. I pushed the buttons on the grinders, filled the filter baskets for the coffee makers. Dark in one, medium roast in the next, and decaf in the third. The aroma of coffee gave my soul a lift.

"Just like back in the States, isn't it?" Jake asked. He was leaning on the counter, looking at my espresso setup. I raised a finger to my lips to shush him.

Aunt Rose stood by the door, her hand on the key to unlock it, and looked back over her shoulder. Outside, several figures waited, silhouetted against the dim streetlight.

"Ready to start our new partnership, dearie?"

"Let them in. It's time to brew!"

2

Six hours later, coffee grounds overflowed from the countertop dump bin and the bin under the counter I kept emptying it into.

"I don't believe I've ever made that many drinks in one shift, not even on Black Friday."

"One more? Please?" Nia said. Her shoulders were slumped, her apron stained with flour, cream, coffee, and who knew what else. Aunt Rose stood next to her, looking as prim and proper as when we began the day.

"How did your apron stay so clean?" My own sported splotches and splatters, though not as bad as Nia's.

"Practice, dearie," she said, humming as she wiped down the counter again. The few customers who remained chatted amongst themselves. Aunt Rose had tried to introduce me to everyone as the day progressed, but my hands stayed busy, tamping fresh grounds, steaming milk, squirting syrup, and all the little things that made me a barista. Not that I could remember all their names. There had been so many people, and they all wanted to shake my hand. I had shaken a couple hundred hands.

"What drink did you want, Nia?"

"Oh! Can I have another caramel marching tornado?"

"You mean caramel macchiato? Coming right up."

I made several, one for each of us, and passed them around. Nia cooed as she held the cup between both of her small hands. Her smile grew wide and tall as she inhaled the aroma.

"Yum!" she breathed after the first sip. "Will you teach me how to make these, Ebrel? Please?"

I laughed, getting used to the British version of my name. The accents of everyone here, even of the Scotsman Red, were so comforting. Words rolled from one syllable to the next, unlike how Americans over-accented syllables to make their point even more apparent.

A yawn escaped me.

"Sorry, still working on my jet lag," I said. "I'll clean the espresso machine and grab a nap before tea time."

"Don't be worrying about tea service, dearie," Aunt Rose said. "Nia's sister will help with that. We'll not be doing your fancy drinks but in the morning. At least not until you get adjusted to our time."

"Oh, thank you!" I leaned in to hug her. She smelled of gingerbread, cinnamon, and roses. "Let me get the station set for tomorrow. I may sleep all day and night."

"Let's see." I opened the cupboard behind my drink station. "We used more beans than I expected. I'll have to make another run downstairs."

"What do you need?" Aunt Rose asked.

"If tomorrow is like today, then three more regular espresso bags, and two decaf. Plus the dark and medium coffee."

I got my machine cleaned while Nia and Aunt Rose cleaned

the tables and made the place presentable for the afternoon tea service.

"Expect more crowds like our rush this morning," Rose said. "The town has been waiting for you and your fancy drink machine. Now they know, and they'll be back every morning. Add in any tourists who stumble upon us, and we will be busy."

I smiled at that. One of the few uses for my special magic was the little surge I put into each drink I made. A little zap to put some extra energy into the espresso and milk. Like Aunt Rose's cookies... or biscuits as they were called here in Britain, I made the drinks had that extra dash of special taste that came with a special touch. Only mine came from the magic I couldn't tell anyone about.

"Let me go grab—" I paused mid-sentence to yawn. "—that coffee, then I'm off to bed."

"Check the cupboard at your station, dearie," Aunt Rose said.

Puzzled, I opened the door. It was chock full of coffee. Exactly the quantity I had requested. I must be exhausted if they had filled the cupboard behind me without my noticing.

Jake and a chicken waited in my room.

"I'm too tired to say much," I said, plopping down on the edge of the bed. "Your twenty-four hours is about finished, isn't it? Sorry. Yesterday was too full of Aunt Rose to get a good chat in with you."

Jake nodded. "You'll see me again in a year."

"Every year," I said and held my hand up. Even though he was another of what my father called my kooky boyfriends, Jake had a special place in my heart.

"I'll miss you, April." He held his hand out, almost touching mine. Only death separated our touch. "Until next year."

He faded from view, and I faded down to my pillow.

THREE HOURS OF BEING DEAD ASLEEP MUST HAVE BEEN enough. I was wide awake.

Downstairs in the kitchen, Aunt Rose planted her hands on her hips. I started back to the café.

"No. You go see the valley, dearie," she said. "I know that look on your face. Just like your mother's. You want to go climb the cliff, don't you?"

"I'll stay and help with tea," I said. "We're partners, and I need to learn that too."

"Not today, dearie. You did awesome this morning. You're like your mother, and she'd be climbing that cliff or the tallest tree she could find."

"Really? Mom was a climber?"

"I saw it in your eyes when we drove in yesterday," Aunt Rose said. "You stared at that cliff the entire way into the valley. I'll make a call and have someone meet you at the top, so you don't get lost on your way back."

"I can find my way. The valley isn't that big." I smiled again and hugged her. "I've got my mobile with me. There's service in the valley, isn't there?"

"Yes, dearie, now go. And have some fun. You earned it."

MY PHONE BUZZED. THE SMARTWATCH, RATHER, WAS vibrating on my wrist. I was more than halfway up the short cliff face but had a hand free. I tapped the accept button on my watch, then searched for another handhold.

"What's happening, Pops?" I said. The earbuds I wore, with special clips to keep them in place, had a noise-cancelling mic built in. He wouldn't be able to hear the wind of the valley.

"Happy birthday, little monkey," Dad's voice sounded in my earbuds. My parents always called on my birthday.

"I'm thirty-six, Pops," I said. My fingers found a crevice and dug in. Half of my weight didn't budge the rock, so I shifted and stared to raise my foot.

"You're still my little monkey, April. Are you climbing now?"

I smiled. "Why wouldn't I be?"

"You drained your trust account again. Where are you now?"

"Wales," I said. Another foothold secured, I pushed up, and my left hand felt for a hold.

"You drained all that money to go to the UK?"

"Not the entire trust," I said.

"No, just your annual payout. What are you up to now?"

"Aunt Rose invited me to come be a partner in her café. I want to bring a love of the perfect espresso to Wales. Aunt Rose says too many Brits still drink instant coffee. I must change that."

There was silence, longer than his usual pauses.

"You're in business with that crazy old bat? Couldn't you find another drifter biker boyfriend to waste the money on?"

"Dad! You only ever brought me to the UK to visit Mom's family once. I was only five. Aunt Rose was sweet then. She still is."

"So she's sucking all of your money to revamp that kitschy run-down dump of a tea room? What did she spend it on, more ugly decor?"

"No," I said. A fight with my father on my birthday was normal. I expected this one. "I spent it on a professional espresso machine for the café. That and a full coffee station. And a top-end roaster that should arrive next week. We're doing Mystic Brews, a custom coffee and teahouse. The only one for twenty miles in any direction."

"Why didn't you stay in the States and start one?"

"I tried that, remember?" It had failed because I'm a much worse businessperson than I am a barista. "Aunt Rose will handle the business stuff, and I'll make the best coffee in Wales. She said she'd been getting requests from tourists for foo-foo drinks. She didn't know what to get or how to use it."

"That crazy old woman! Make sure to check her figures, your inventory, and your bank balance at least daily. I don't trust her."

My handhold broke free. A surge of magic anchored my feet and left hand to the wall. I sucked in a breath.

"Honey? You okay?"

"Yeah. Sorry, a rock was loose. I'm fine." My fingers kept exploring. There was another hold, a few inches farther, that felt sturdy. I popped some magic through my right hand to make sure the rock would stay put. I always let my mind drift and forgot to do that when I had a fight with my father.

"Why do you have to climb? Never mind. There's a reason I called you monkey when you were little. I should know better."

"Thanks, Dad," I said. A few more handholds and I'd be at the top of the cliff.

"Thanks for what? Giving you money every year?"

"No. For caring." He did, too. He was, however, too gruff, too business oriented to show it. He was a tough guy when he was in business mode. The only time he wasn't was... well... never.

"I'll put ten grand in the emergency fund," Dad added. "For when you realise how crazy your mother's family is. Call or email, and I'll have Cynthia release it to your trust account."

"I love you, too, Pops. Thanks for thinking of me today."

"You're welcome, monkey. Call me if you need something."

The call clicked to silence. He probably only had five minutes on his calendar for the call. I pulled myself past the lip of the rock face and rolled into a sitting position, my legs dangling over the edge. I tapped the face of my watch to check the call record. Four fifty-seven. That was Pops.

He'd set aside time on my birthday, like he always did. Pops never understood why I preferred guys who were more free spirited. He didn't like Jake and hadn't been sad when Jake died three years ago. But he let me cry on his shoulder.

Fifteen minutes after I arrived, he took a call in the other room. A merger he was working on. That was my dad. Ever the businessman.

❧ 3 ❧

"**N**ice view, isn't it?"

My head jerked around. Magic shot to the tips of my fingers. I held it in check. Didn't want to give my nature away. It was there in case I had to slap some sense into the guy. Should have looked before I put my back to the treeline. Too many jerks had snuck up on me in the past.

"Who are you?" I rolled to my feet and shifted away from the edge.

A tall, thin blond man sat on a folded camp stool, a large notepad on his lap.

"Can you step a few paces to your left?" He squinted and cocked his head to see past me. "The light is perfect on the other side of the valley, and I'm trying to get the tree shapes before the sun drops too low.

"Artist?"

"Yes, please move. You make a better wall than a window."

His accent had that same rolling Welsh sound I was getting used to.

I did as he suggested. The magic I had called ebbed away. I hoped I didn't need it against this guy.

"Hi, I'm April," I said but didn't offer my hand. I'd been around enough artistic types to know he wouldn't budge until he finished what he was working on. Instead, I pulled my earbuds out and secured them in the neckband. The mouthpiece for my hydration backpack was clipped to a strap. I raised it and took a sip. Then another.

"Do you mind if I look?"

"Not at all," he said. "You're Ebrel, Rhosyn's niece, correct?" He pronounced Aunt Rose's regular Welsh name, with the guttural Hr sound, reversing the Rh as it was spelled. No matter, in Rose, the R was the same as in America. Welsh accents were fun to listen to, and I was starting to pick up the lilt in my own accent.

"Yes. The joys of a small town. Everyone knows everyone's business."

"You'd be surprised." The other side of the valley was sketched across the width of the paper.

"Nice work," I said. "You are?"

"Io," he said, pronouncing it more like Eye-Oh in his Welsh accent.

"Sounds like that's short for something?"

"Ioworth, actually," he said. This time the name sounded more like 'Yahwurth' with the accent on the latter syllable. "Edward in English. Io, with the English pronunciation for short. You don't speak Welsh?"

"Nope. My mother didn't teach me much by the time she left. I can say diolch and a few phrases. Said she even chose the…" I paused trying to remember the various dialects in Britain, "the Cornish version of April. She said Americans always have problems with the double-Ls at the end of the Welsh form.

Dad insisted they use with the American version on my birth certificate."

"Ebrill... April," Io said. The ending sound was more of a mixed L and H said together. "Simple to us Cymry to pronounce. But Americans get tongue-tied outside of their version of English."

"She had a brother named Eddie, but she never called him Io or Ioworth. Your dad doesn't have the same name, does he?"

"No, my parents are passed," he said. "Rhosyn asked me to keep an eye on you, make sure you didn't get lost on your first day in the valley."

"I told her I didn't need watching..." I didn't like the idea of a babysitter. Especially not one who looked like he was in his early twenties. I understood her concern, though.

"We've only got about an hour of daylight left. Less in the valley. Do you want me to walk you down to the village?"

I glanced at the cliff face. My plan had been to go back the way I'd come, but walking with a friend of Aunt Rose's seemed safer, given the dropping sun.

"I brought a torch," Io said. He folded his camp stool and stored it and his sketchpad in his backpack.

"And matches to light the torch?"

"Torch..." He laughed. "...is British for a battery-powered light."

"Ah, thanks," I said. "This American girl has a lot to learn about her new home."

"You're staying, then?" He waved me to the path through the trees.

"I hope so," I said, then I shrugged. "America never felt like home."

The sun had dropped low enough that twilight hit the valley floor. A light fog rolled in as the air cooled.

"This really is Misty Valley," I said. Aunt Rose had told me the name in Welsh, Cwm Aneglur, meant hidden or misty valley.

A furry orange shape scampered out of the treeline and walked next to Io.

"Hey, Punkin," Io said. The cat looked at him. I swear it winked.

"You can breathe," Io said to me. "You don't have to hold your breath."

"I'm allergic to cats," I said, then turned my head away from the orange tabby. I sucked in a quick breath. Maybe I could escape an attack.

The road had been rising and hid the village. When we crested the rise, I paused and stared. The village was beautiful. Below us, fairy lights danced on the breeze. The plants themselves glowed with inner lights. Beautiful against the twilight blue of the evening. This, however, wasn't normal lighting.

One of the fairy lights zipped at us. It was some sort of bug? No...

A real fairy. A girl, three inches tall, with gossamer wings, dressed in a teal dress, darted right at me.

"Ebrel!" Her voice was familiar. "It's me, Nia! Will you make me another caramel tornado?"

"What in blazes?" I looked at Io, then down at Punkin.

"Welcome to Cwm Tylwyth," the cat said and winked at me.

"Which means?" I sputtered, still awestruck by the little Nia in front of me. It didn't register that the cat had spoken.

"Valley of the Fae," Nia squeaked.

"It's a modern translation, and we've simplified it best as we can," Io said. "Welcome home, niece."

laid a gem on the table. From it, a miniature image of my mother arose. Long braided golden-red hair. Hippy beads hung around her neck, and she had long, dangling earrings—the Celtic Tree of Life stamped into a cheap piece of brass.

"Aunt Rose says you passed all the tests, today, sweetie," Mom said. "I'm so proud of you!"

"Tests?"

"Everyone you shook hands with had a charm they were using," Aunt Rose added. "You scored very high on the test. Near the level of the queen herself."

"Is Britain's queen..."

"No. Her Royal Majesty is a different person from Her Grace, Queen of the Fae. We use those words in that order to differentiate whom we are discussing." Aunt Rose gave me one of her soft smiles. "I, too, am proud of you."

"I don't feel like I did anything except make a bunch of drinks. More drinks than I've ever made."

"And," my mom continued, "Aunt Rose said you put a zap of magic into each one. Everyone in the café today was magic sensitive. They could tell." Mom turned towards my aunt. "I believe it's time, Rose."

Aunt Rose stood. She fished in her right sleeve this time and drew forth a stick as thick as my little finger. The tip and handle were dark red, like a ruby, but cloudy, not a gemstone.

"From one fae to another, the magic is passed," Aunt Rose said. "From mother to daughter, the wand is gifted. Do you, Ebrel Dymestl, swear to use your powers to benefit our people, our lands, and our society?"

"Of course I do," I said. "I've always done that. Even when I thought I was the only one with magic." Aunt Rose held the wand out towards me, thick end first.

"Welcome," Aunt Rose said when my fingers closed around the handle. The stick vibrated, and the red at either end glowed and turned green. "You are kin. You are Tylwyth Teg. You are my niece Ebrel of the Storms, Ebrel Dymestl."

A jolt of something crackled between that cat and me. Almost like a spark of static electricity. Only there was more than just electricity in the spark.

"Yes!" Punkin called out. "A century from now, I get my old form back." He started doing a four-paw side-to-side, front-to-back celebratory dance in the table. I stifled a giggle as his back end swayed to music only he could imagine.

"My apologies, dearie," Aunt Rose added. "My sister tied his curse to serving one of us. The spell she placed on him just connected you two. You're the first one of our family to qualify for the unfortunate privilege of Punkin as your familiar."

✣　4　✤

Oof!

Whatever landed on me wasn't gentle, nor welcome at 4:30 in the morning.

"Wake up, Ebrel!"

"Punkin! Go away!" I pulled the pillow over my head. My first day with a familiar, and he was already annoying me. The alarm on the bedside table went off, and a cat paw reached under the pillow to swat my nose.

"Aunt Rose said you need to be awake this morning," Punkin's voice plowed its way under my soft, fluffy head cave. "The pixies are looking to bring tourists in today."

I tossed the pillow off and righted myself, rubbing sleep out of my eyes. My first day as a newly minted witch in the Misty Valley was off to a lethargic start. I wanted to sleep. I still wasn't over my jet lag.

"Didn't we have tourists in the café yesterday?"

"No, those were all fae and other magicals," Punkin said and head-butted me.

"I'm up! Give a girl a moment."

"We did," he said. "You hit the snooze twice."

My head swung to the clock, which said 4:50, not 4:30. Oh boy! I was close to missing my five a.m. set-up time.

"Wait," I said and laid back down. "I already prepped the station. All I have to do is turn it on and let it warm up."

"Eeeeeeeebrellllllllll!" a tiny voice cried, and the buzz of wings flitted from one side of my head to the other. "Time for a caramel tornado! Get up!" She grabbed hold of my T-shirt. "Don't make me grow big just to get you out of bed. I'm chuffed just thinking about your drinks."

"Ugh! You too?" I rose again. "Let me hit the loo and the bath."

"Yaaaaaaay!" Nia squealed and zipped away.

Once I made it downstairs, I was surprised to see about a dozen people already in the café. They seemed familiar. Red was there, and Io. They ranged from men ready to work in offices or drive a truck. I mean a lorry, or whatever a truck is called in Britain. A man sat in the back in a white shirt with an emblem above the pocket. Towards the front of the store, a table of young women, thin, with bright-coloured highlights in their hair, watched me intently. Their eyes showed their anticipation.

"Pixies?" I asked Nia. She wore her teal apron. Her hair highlights matched the apron.

"Of course they are," Nia said and started introducing them. My head was swimming with all their names. I'd be lucky to remember even one of them for five minutes.

"You all go to the same stylist?" I asked. "Your hair seems to have the same theme, but different colours."

"No, silly," Nia said. "Pixies have coloured hair like ours. It changes with our moods."

"So what's the bad colour?"

"Red," they all said at once.

"Pink is fine, and orange is still a happy colour," Nia added.

"Me mum used to go scarlet. When that happened, every pixie in twenty leagues hid."

I giggled. Nia shot me a worried look.

"Me mum would laugh, then pluck your wings if you did that in front of her."

"I don't have wings," I said and giggled again.

"She'd magic some on you just to pluck them." All the pixies at the table nodded.

"Can we have a caramel tornado?" one of them asked. "Your aunt Rhosyn said we could come in early before the mundanes showed up."

Six caramel macchiatos wouldn't take too long. That included the one for Nia.

"Come with me, pixie girl." I waved Nia along. "If your friends are going to show up every morning, you need to learn how to make these."

"You mean better than last night?"

"Anything would be better than what you did last night," I said. "Did you drink it?"

"Well, you left it on the table..."

"Do pixies eat a lot of sugar? Like hummingbirds need to?"

"Of course, silly. That's why we have so much energy."

"And caffeine?"

"We don't need it," she said. "The sugar is what we crave."

"Espresso won't hurt them, dearie," Aunt Rose called from the kitchen. "Nia, go bring the rest of the pastries out. Make sure the case is full."

I waved at Red and Io and slid behind the counter. A stack of newspapers lay there, the top one flipped over. Fairly thin, and not the London Times. Story on the bottom of the page was about an athlete who had gone missing a year ago.

"Mystic Mystery. Interesting name for a paper."

"Diolch," one man at the table said. "You'll notice that the business profile of this little café is top of the fold."

"Wow! You even got a photo of me working the steamer, and I don't look like a troll."

"Definitely not a troll," Red said. "Been a few years since we had one in the valley. Reminds me. I need ta go check the bridges by the waterfall and make sure they're still in good repair. Since we lost Bob, no one has been taking care of them."

I pressed the tamper on the first portafilter of ground espresso. No need to twist it, though. Too much polish, and the water didn't want to go through the grounds right away.

"Bob was the maintenance guy?" I asked.

"He was our troll. You probably won't remember, Miss Dymestl, I'm Mayor Yardley," Said the tall thin man with an equally thin moustache.

I had the milk pitcher under the steamer wand and let it work its magic on the cream to get a layer of froth. Then I shifted the pitcher up to mix and heat the milk.

"Thanks, Mayor. I remember."

"So glad to have you in our little valley." The way his eyes slid around, like he was a rodent waiting on a hawk to grab him, and the moist handshake that went on too long, told me he was a politician who aspired higher than he was cut out for. I'd met several like him when my father insisted I work in his office in New York.

"Thank you, Mister Mayor."

"You are most welcome, Ebrel," he said and finally let go of my hand. "I may call you Ebrel? You look put off by it."

"That's fine," I said. I caught myself right before I wiped my hand on my apron. "I'm still not used to my British names. Ebrel is close to April. But Dymestl, what does that mean?"

"Dymestl is our family name, dearie," Aunt Rose said. "It means a heavy storm, a tempest, in English."

"My mother, with a Welsh surname for storm, married David Ignatius Storm III? How appropriate..."

Caramel waited in the paper cups. The milk for the first three macchiatos was almost up to temp, so I started the espresso. My machine was a double-sized, so I could tamp a second cup's worth as the first one brewed. I was an efficient little barista.

"First set, here you pixies go."

"Don't forget to ring them up, Nia," Aunt Rose called. "If they do well, we'll make tomorrow's round on the house."

"Pixies use money?"

"Of course," Mayor Yardley said. "We may be fae and magicals, but we're not heathens. Our little village needs to coexist with the rest of Wales and Britain. I'm working to get a road race here in our little valley to bring in a wave of racing tourists. We'll call it the Mystic Grand Prix! If you will excuse me, miss, I've got some calls to make. The HF Racing Commission is here for a meeting in a few days. Very important decisions to make about the race."

I gave him a polite smile, then breathed a sigh as the door shut behind the mayor. The gent who seemed connected to the newspaper stepped up as I pushed the other three cups towards the last of the pixies.

"Miss Dymestl, Roger Billingsley, owner of the Mystic Mystery. Most pleased to make your acquaintance." He didn't look as old as my father, but I'd learned last night that "old" in this valley wasn't what it seemed like elsewhere. "My apologies for our mayor. Unfortunately, no one else wants the job."

I shook his hand, then turned to wash mine.

"My apologies, health regulations."

"No need to apologise, Miss Dymestl," he said. "You wore that sink out yesterday, shaking everyone's hands. I was one of the few who didn't bother you. Journalistic objectivity and all."

"You arrived too late to get a detection crystal," Aunt Rose said and slid another tray of pastries into the glass-fronted case. "I had to put a sani-towel out for you, dearie. You ran through an entire pump bottle of hand soap."

"Don't worry, I won't tell the mayor," the newspaperman said. "He's also head of the health department."

"And bridge maintenance, and the pwca snow removal units, and..." Red said. "He tells us every time he can."

"Five minutes till we open," Aunt Rose called. "I see several others waiting outside. If any of you lot wants one of Ebrel's Mystic Brews coffee drinks, get it now before the door spell unlocks."

The morning whizzed by again in a stampede of people needing coffee, or the "foo-foo drinks" as Aunt Rose still called them. I wondered if half the pixies in Britain must have showed up looking for a "caramel tornado." We'd need to get more caramel syrup this week. I barely had time to take a break and flip open the paper. The story above the fold was a glowing report of my first day on the job at the café.

Io popped back into the kitchen where I was taking my break. He had been with me when I discovered the valley was full of fae, and that I was one of them. Not only that, he was my uncle and appeared to be only in his early twenties. I had just turned thirty-six and looked no older than he did.

"You'll have a line of customers when you go back," he said. "Some pixies found us a caravan load of American tourists. They're overjoyed at the mention of coffee instead of tea." He reached into his sleeve. He plucked his own wand out and tapped the paper with it. His wand glowed green, just like mine.

"Touch the page like this and think of fae," he said. "That activates the magical mystery of the Mystery."

"Ah!" The photo of me wasn't just a still. I was moving, like a video. The letters shifted around, and a new story appeared.

"Daughter of Jasmine Dymestl Passes Majority Test, Gets Wand," said the headline. The photo shifted to one of me and Aunt Rose when she passed the wand to me and everyone applauded. Mayor Yardley was front and center and winked at the camera. The pixies, led by Nia and her blue-streaked hair, buzzed and flitted around me.

"Why didn't I notice the pixies' hair with those bright streaks of colour yesterday?"

"You hadn't come into your majority yet," Io said and slid his wand back into his sleeve. "Now that you have your wand, you can see the magic around you."

"You're as bad as Aunt Rose." Like any grandmotherly aged woman, she always seemed to have a tissue and other oddities tucked up her sleeves.

"I'll show you the magic on how to store it there, once your shift ends. Where is it now?"

"My wand? On the chest of drawers in my room," I said and pointed at my attire. The same as the day before, just cleaner versions. Yoga pants and a long top, but I had added a short skirt. "No pockets, so I wasn't sure where to keep it."

"Is Punkin there? He should know not to leave your wand unattended."

I shrugged, then nodded. "He curled up on the pillow when I came down. I've got so much to learn about all this magic stuff."

"You need training. Most of the children in our community get that from their parents," Io said. "We heard about the custody battle your mum had with your father about you. Your father isn't fae, so you didn't learn any of this. I'll be your mentor this year since I owe my sister at least that much. She looked out for me my first century."

"Century? How old is she? Or you?" Another of those little facts that everyone kept dropping on me, making my head swim.

"I'm 261. Sis is seventy-seven years older. That's how often fae women can bear a child."

The math made my head hurt. "Three hundred thirty-eight? I hope I look as good as she does when I'm fifty."

"Silly girl," Aunt Rose said from the door to the main room. "You'll live at least twenty times that long. Unless you don't get out here soon. We've got about a dozen drink orders ready for you."

"A dozen is a number I can handle," I told Io. "You must explain more this afternoon about the three-hundred-years parts."

$$\mathfrak{P} \quad 5 \quad \mathfrak{P}$$

"Hi, April," a familiar voice said.

"Hey," I muttered and continued wiping down my espresso machine. We'd had a late rush. The pixies had been out flying, looking for people on holiday, making sure they knew about Mystic Brews. The locked door and a sign that read "closed till tea time" gave us a respite. Only magical creatures could enter now, and they knew, Aunt Rose said, to come in through the kitchen door.

I dumped another bag of beans in the grinder and twisted the lid to seal it. A single feather drifted down to land on the counter next to it.

My eyes jerked up.

"What are you doing here?"

Jake shrugged. "I always hang around you."

"Why can I see and hear you today? That shouldn't be."

"Ebrel, dearie," Aunt Rose called. "To whom are you speaking?"

I swallowed and looked at Jake, with his ghostly leather jacket covered in chicken feathers.

"My ex-boyfriend," I said. Coming clean to her was a gamble. I realised there was so much about the world of magic I didn't understand.

"Oh, that young ghost with the chickens? He's such a nice boy. Pity he died so young."

"Why are you here?" I hissed again. Something wasn't right. I had always been able to see ghosts, though only on the anniversary day of their death. I got one day a year to spend with Jake. His death day was also my birthday. And now the day I came into my witch majority and got my wand.

"Wait... you can see him too?"

I felt Aunt Rose at my side.

"Magic, my dear," she said and patted her apron pockets. "Now, wherever did I put my spectacles?" They were perched atop her head. Jake being here distracted me from pointing them out.

"Why can I see him today? Yesterday was his death day." This worried me. I wasn't sure how the change in time zones from America would affect that.

"I'm afraid you've got your mother's abilities, too," Aunt Rose said. She wrapped an arm around me for a side hug. "You tested high on all the magic charms, so you've got strong witch ability too. Your mother could only get a few of them to tingle, and none to glow."

"What's all that mean? Why can I see and hear Jake, but the rest of ... everyone here can't?"

"I've got magic spectacles that help me see all sorts of things," she said. "Spirits, demons trying to hide. That's why I didn't worry about your friend yesterday. Io spoke to you about training? With you being in the States and away from your mother, you need to learn the basics we teach our children. After that, I'll take over your training."

"Ah... so I can see and hear ghosts, but no one else can. I'm a baby in the magic world, and I have potential to be some super witch?" I leaned back against the counter, rubbing my temples. "This is a little much for a girl who just wanted to be the best barista in the UK."

"Lattes and magic, dearie," Aunt Rose said and tucked her spirit-seeing spectacles back in her sleeve. "You'll be the best at both once I get you trained."

"How long will that take? I need to train Nia on lattes and macchiatos, too."

"A few decades should get you wanding equal to anyone in Misty Valley. After that, we'll take your training into the very advanced stages."

"A few decades? I'll be in my fifties..." I thought about Io, who'd just said he was over two hundred. "Oh, I guess that doesn't matter..."

"Have fun with Io today, dearie," she said. "I'm bringing on Mia, another of the pixies, to help with mornings and afternoon tea. Can you train Nia on your foo-foo drinks tomorrow morning?"

"I tried this morning, but the rush was too much. You pulled her back to the counter every time I tried. Each time, she forgot what I just said. I'm not sure she can focus long enough to learn all the drinks. She seems a little flighty," I said.

Nia heard me and spun around.

"Thank you! All pixies love to fly! I'm very good at spins and twists when I fly."

"Yes, dear," Aunt Rose said and patted my hand. "She'll be fine. Pixies are very task oriented and learn quickly. Unfortunately, they don't task-switch well. She needs to be either at the counter or on the espresso machine."

"I'll learn to make drinks as good as you?"

"With some practice, yes," I said.

Nia almost squealed, clapping her hands together.

"That means you will take the pixie hour in the morning," Aunt Rose said. "If we provide those caramel drinks–"

"Macchiatos," I interjected and stopped Nia from calling them tornados again.

"I have no idea where she learned that word. We call such storms twisters here," Aunt Rose said. "If we give her friends the macchiatos, then they'll be our ambassadors, bringing tourists into our little valley."

"You want tourists here?"

"During the day, of course," Aunt Rose said. "We fae are just as much a part of the British economy as the mundanes. Our craftspeople, and artists like Io, need to sell their handiworks."

"Aren't you worried they'll find out about the magic?"

"Not at all, dearie," she said. "We've been doing this for generations. When I learned that you excelled at this espresso thing, we had a town meeting and decided to invite you back specifically to help us grow. We needed to test you, anyway. Bringing you back seemed the safest way."

"Now we both get to help each other. Nice."

Punkin wandered down, carrying my wand in his mouth.

"Blech! Wash that occasionally," he said when he dropped it on the counter next to the latest copy of the Mystic Mystery. "It tastes like old witch sleeve."

I groaned.

"Of all the familiars, I get a smart-alec cat."

"Pwca," Punkin said. Aunt Rose said his normal size was about that of the orange tabby cat form he was now in.

"If you don't want to be a cat, go talk to Her Grace," Aunt Rose said. "If you ask very nicely, she might reverse the curse."

"Only you might not want to ralph chewed-up coffee beans on her dress again." I laughed when Punkin stuck his tongue out at me. It looked cute on his orange cat face.

"The last time I tried to plead for forgiveness, she threatened to have me neutered," Punkin said.

"April," Jake said. He floated to the counter by the newspapers. "I want you to meet a friend of mine."

"Wait? Ghosts have friends?"

"I just met him this morning," Jake said.

"Who's she talking to?" Punkin asked Aunt Rose.

"Her boyfriend's ghost. She has her mother's ability."

"I thought I smelled chickens. Did she date a chicken?" Punkin jumped back behind the counter and started nosing under the espresso station.

"Are you going to dump all of these grounds? What a waste."

"You keep your nose out of there, stinker," I said. "I don't want you barfing up a coffee hairball on my clothes."

"April! Can you focus on my friend, please. It's important." Jake wasn't normally impatient.

"Sorry, Jake."

He waved his friend forward. A tall man. British, prim and proper. White slacks and a collared shirt. He held a cap in his hands. It was similar to a baseball cap, but not exactly. Shorter brim, and made of wool or felt.

"Most delighted to meet you, Miss Dymestl," he said with a slight bow to his head. "Pardon me for not offering my hand."

"Quite all right," I said. Even if I could see and talk to ghosts, and they looked solid most of the time, it didn't mean they could touch anything. I might as well shake hands with a cloud. "Should I know you? You seem familiar."

"The paper," the man said. "Turn it over. Your arrival bumped me below the fold."

"World's Most-Cricket Cricket Player Still Missing," the headline read.

"Sir Reginald Dewsberry," I said, reading his name underneath the photo of him. I remembered to touch the paper with my wand. The tip glowed green, and I felt a pulse of energy leak through it.

His portrait shifted to a highlight reel of the same fellow pitching a ball towards another player, also in white, holding a wooden bat down by his feet.

"What a shame, dearie," Aunt Rose said. She was consolidating trays of sweets and pastries in the glass case to make room for the afternoon's fresh supply. "He's been missing almost a year now. Right after he retired from cricket. One of the best fae to ever play, and also one of the nicest."

"My fellow players all seemed to believe so," Sir Reginald said. "I just tried to play the sport as best I could. Anything else wouldn't be cricket!"

"I do hope he's just run off somewhere," Nia said. "He was always so nice when he came to the valley."

"No, he's dead," I said.

"I need help to discover who did me in," he said. "Your man here"—he waved at Jake—"said you might be willing to lend assistance."

Aunt Rose stared at me. She fished around in her sleeves again.

"Ebrel?"

"Murdered," I said.

Aunt Rose patted her head and found her spectacles. She gave them a wipe with a corner of her apron. When she put her glasses on, she gave a little jerk of her head when she saw him.

"Sir Reginald," she said. "Is it true?"

He nodded for her benefit.

"Nia, call Inspector Jones, tell him I said to drop everything and get here now."

recognise we fae, nor ghosts, as ethnic groups, nor magic and spirits as credible sources. You can, however, provide testimony to lead us to your body and evidence about your death. Do you remember how you died?"

"Now that the death amnesia, as the spirits call it, has worn off, yes," Sir Reginald said. "Just not why. I suspect there may have been some... let us say non-cricket behaviour from someone at the fete."

Again, I relayed the words, and the ghost nodded when I finished.

"Start with your demise," the inspector prompted. "Where and when?"

"On my drive down from the manor," Sir Reginald said. "I switched to proper tea an hour or so before I had to drive. I turned down many a request for 'just one more shot of whiskey' with the Scottish players. The Australians also tried to pass on more of their beer. When I declined several times, they said they would have one more round in my honour. I suspect they had several more rounds, despite my apologies. And our French brethren of the sport tried to insist that I had to try their best Bordeaux. None persuaded me. I will not imbibe and drive. The new sports car I allowed myself to indulge in upon my retirement awaited me. I longed to get it onto the curving mountain roads down from the manor and see just how well it handled."

"Sir Reginald was also one of our most qualified amateur racers in the fae road courses," the inspector explained. "I do not doubt his driving ability. Please, continue." He waved towards Sir Reginald, making more notes on his pad as we went.

"On my trip down the mountain, my vision became blurred, and my breathing shallow, as though I were asleep. I sought a place to pull off the road. The mountain road was too narrow with no shoulders, though. I looked for the turn-off to head back to this valley but drove on by it somehow. That put me on the longer, more winding road towards Shrewsbury."

"That turn-off is easy to miss," the inspector said. "Only one faded sign. With Bob gone, we haven't gotten around to replacing the ageing road signage. Continue, please, Sir Reginald."

"My car drove on when the road took a sharp curve. I don't remember flying off."

"We searched all along both the road to Misty Valley, and towards the main motorway, and didn't find any marks of skidding."

"Doubtful that you would have," Sir Reginald said. "I was barely conscious and couldn't keep my eyes open. The car crashed and bounced, then nothing. I stood in a ravine, under an outcropping, staring at what was left of my beautiful new sportster. She'll never drive again, I'm afraid."

"So you walked away from the wreck?" The inspector made notes.

"Not at all, I'm afraid. After the crash, I was just as you see me now." Sir Reginald waited until I passed that on. "Miss, I beg you not to go down with the inspector. What little is left of me in that wreck is not fit for a lady's eyes. Promise me you will remain away. It would grieve me to no end if my death were to cause you anguish."

"You're very sweet, Sir Reginald," I said. "You are correct. I would prefer to leave such matters to the authorities."

"I'll need you to come with us, however, far enough to interpret and identify the location, Miss Dymestl," the inspector said. He turned back to the ghost.

"Do you have any idea why you were so fatigued or blacked out on the drive?"

"No idea at all, good inspector," the ghost shook his head. "It was a beautiful night. I remember the clock on the dash read just past midnight. The earl and lady do like their late-night parties, so I had rested up for it. But the open road called to me. I wanted to give my new sportster a challenge in the evening when there was little traffic."

"When we find your wreck, I'll have toxicology run tests on your remains," the inspector added. "Something sounds off about all of this. Do you remember anyone there at the party who wanted to do you harm? Anyone with past grudges?"

"Oh, my dear inspector," Sir Reginald said, straightening his shoulders, "those are the men of cricket. Need I remind you of the spirit of cricket. We are all professionals and cared only about the game and maintaining its reputation."

"I've met many of those players," Inspector Jones said. "I don't hold the same opinion of some of their characters as you do."

"Reginald! There you are!" a shrill voice shouted from across the café. A strong odour of the sea and a pile of seaweed assaulted my senses. I turned towards the voice. The inspector did too, after he saw me move. No one else had even blinked. The newcomer was another ghost.

"I noticed the look on Sir Reginald's face," the inspector whispered. "Who is that and what is she saying?"

"Mother..." Sir Reginald breathed, exasperation haunting his tone.

"I'm sorry," I said to the woman. She looked like an older version of Aunt Rose but with harder lines in her spectral face. Jewellery of various sorts adorned her. Rings on every finger, several necklaces and pendants. Earrings that I'd call gawdy on a good day. Today, I wasn't feeling that generous. Ostentatious, perhaps. Definitely tilted toward tasteless.

"This is my café. Can I help you?" I said. In the past, I'd found that a stern approach and announcement of authority was best. Since Aunt Rose couldn't see her, I had to take the lead.

"This is Rose's café, sweetie," the ghost said flippantly. "Reginald! I went looking for you at the cricket pitch and didn't find you. I thought we'd watch another match today."

"His mother," I whispered to the inspector.

"Is that Betrys Dewsberry?" Aunt Rose's voice carried through the café from behind the counter. "She hasn't been around since she and her husband had their spat and destroyed four blocks down in Swansea."

"Hmmfph! Now that Reginald has passed, I finally get to spend time with him. I only found out a few weeks ago," the female ghost said. She wore a long floor-length dress, aquamarine in colour, and her grey hair waved in an unearthly breeze that only she seemed affected by.

"Betrys is a selkie, Ebrel," Aunt Rose called. "She's trouble. Watch out for her."

Sir Reginald's mother ignored Aunt Rose.

"My boy! Why didn't you come to the game?"

"Mother." Sir Reginald stood. "This is Inspector Jones, and this young lady is Ebrel Dymestl, daughter of Jasmine and niece to Miss Rose."

"Delighted," the ghost selkie said in a tone that made me think she was anything but. "Come now, Reginald. You're missing the match."

"Not now, Mother. It's time I was laid to rest. I owe it to the fans and players of the game. Too many of them are still worried. You heard the announcer at the last match. The poor man almost begged for information about me."

"He came to see me." My tone was nearing exasperation. The ghostly woman was getting on my nerves, and she'd only been here half a minute so far.

"You can hear us?" Reginald's mother looked at me.

"She can, just like her mother," Reginald said. "We'll go to the next match. Right now, I want to help the inspector so he can let the fans know what happened to me."

"That's my son," she said, turning towards me. "Always looking out for his fans first." She patted him on the shoulder.

"Do as you need to, dear," she said. "We've got all eternity to see the matches. Missing this one will be fine." She looked back my way.

"Thank you, miss, for helping him. And thank the inspector as well. It's troubled me that my boy was left to rot in that cave. If I weren't already passed, I would have keeled over from the sight of him."

With that, she flipped in the air and swam towards the window. Her gown rolled and flapped as she sailed through the solid wall. One of the cups on the table next to the window rocked from the turbulence she created.

Sir Reginald collapsed into his chair and put his head in his hands. "After decades of not knowing her... I was only five when she and father had that deadly tiff. Forgive me."

I sat in silence. Inspector Jones kept scratching away at his notes while Sir Reginald stared after the ghost of Betrys Dewsberry.

"She's my mother, even if I didn't know her as I grew. We've only been reunited for a few of your weeks, and I'm still getting used to her. She is so difficult." He stared at the window where she had disappeared.

"Please don't tell anyone I said that, Miss Dymestl. It's not cricket."

$\mathscr{H}$ 7 $\mathscr{R}$

Io waited at the counter with Aunt Rose when Inspector Jones finished his questions.

"I surmise that I won't be giving you lessons this morning?"

"Ahh... I suspected that you might be shy of instruction," Owain said. "Perhaps you can drive Miss Dymestl and Sir Reginald to the Valley Overlook and wait for me there?"

Io nodded.

"I need to contact the Gnarly Wreckers and Recovery and get some magical muscle for the retrieval," Jones added. "That should give you time to work in some basics for Miss Dymestl."

"Call me April, or Ebrel, please, Inspector."

He nodded and held out his hand. "Then I'm Owain, or at most, Inspector Owain."

Out in the carpark, Io lead me to his vehicle.

"Oooh! A Mini!" I started to head towards the right side.

"Do you mind if I drive?" he said.

"Silly me. It will take some time to remember the steering wheel is on the other side of the car."

"And please, miss," Sir Reginald added, "remember to look right first, then left. I've seen too many tourists almost end up on this side of the afterlife when they step into traffic."

"You two ride in the back," I said.

"Two?" Io asked.

"Looks like my ex is coming along, too." Jake and Sir Reginald didn't need the doors. They slid into the back of Io's metallic blue car, ignoring the glass and metal.

"Sir Reginald is in with us?" Io asked. A grin lit up his cheeks, and his eyes had a sparkle I hadn't seen in him before. However, I'd only known him two days.

Io pushed a button on the dash. The engine snarled. Not the usual whine and purr of a car—a real snarl.

"Oh, good show," Sir Reginald said. "Ask him what model of demon he's got, please, miss."

"Only a category 2.3," Io said when I asked. "However, I had the engine built with a full racing-grade 4.5 containment cauldron."

"Which means what?" Normal engine talk confused me. Jake loved to talk motorcycles and cubic centimetres and drive sprockets. My eyes glazed over as soon as I heard any of those terms.

"Just listen to the car," Io said. He eased us out of the parking spot and onto the narrow village road. "I need to get out into the valley, then I'll open it up." He touched another button on the dash. I felt something slither on my right shoulder and jerked away.

"Relax. It's a racing harness." Another belt slid down Io's chest, and the normal lap and shoulder belt shifted positions on both of us. Even the headrest and seat behind me was shifting. I now had a belt over each shoulder buckled across my belly. The headrest wrapped forward and around to minimise whiplash in a wreck.

"What is it about men and fast cars?"

"And bikes," Jake said from the back seat. The ghosts didn't have harnesses or belts. They didn't need them since they could poof around from place to place.

A few moments later, we passed the sign at the edge of the village. "Diolch!" it read in Welsh. I didn't get the rest of the words. Underneath that, in English, the translation read "Thank you for visiting Misty Valley. We hope you return soon."

A glow appeared in front of Io. It looked like the heads-up display of glowing squiggles and gauges that movie pilots got in the spaceship cockpits.

"I've got four leagues of clear roads," Io said. "I'll show you what this little demon can do."

The acceleration pressed me back into my seat. That was definitely a growl coming from the engine compartment in front of us.

"Why do I smell brimstone?"

"Demons," Io said. His steering wheel had shifted to a smaller shape, one I assumed was more racing appropriate. He made small adjustments as we zoomed along the winding road and began climbing the side of the valley.

"What? You mean a real demon is inside that little engine?"

"Oh, the demons are actually large. The one in my cauldron is at least as big as this Mini."

"Well, okay, then." I was confused. "How does a critter as large as the car fit into only the engine compartment?"

"Magic," Io said. "Better get used to hearing that. Most of what you'll see and hear for the next few months will be about magic. My sister really didn't teach you much about us, did she?"

"She never had time," I said. "Dad got the courts to agree to only supervised visits due to her mental state. I learned to never tell Pops I could see and hear ghosts. He'd have had me in a loony bin and blamed Mom."

"That's why Jasmine is out in the desert," Io said. "Your father drove her away from you, and she couldn't come back here to all the ghosts that kept talking to her." He looked into his mirror in between taking some hard turns too fast for my taste. "How's the ride back there, people that I can neither see nor hear?"

"Most delightful," Sir Reginald said. "Please tell your uncle that I'm enjoying this."

I passed that on and grabbed the handle on the door. I hadn't liked it when Jake used to race when I was on the back of his bike. This reminded me too much of the few times he had goosed his bike with me on it.

Several more hairpin turns took us higher. Eventually, Io slowed the Mini and crept to a stop sign. He turned left at the T.

"Can we go at a normal pace now?" My knuckles were white and my palms sweaty.

"I'm sorry, Ebrel." Io brought his speed back down to what I considered fast but reasonable for a local driver on curving roads. "My desire to show off made me forget about your lack of experience in the racing world."

"My apologies as well, miss," Sir Reginald said.

"Don't be too nice to her," Jake chimed in. "I've been trying to teach her what a thrill speed is. I was finally getting through to her when that darn opossum waddled in front of me."

"No, you weren't getting through to me," I shot back. "Sorry," I said to Io. "The ghostly gallery are giving me pointers on how to like racing. Especially Jake."

"How much farther?" Io asked.

"Another half a mile, turn onto the road to Shrewsbury," Sir Reginald said. "After another half a mile on, there's a bit of a gravel verge there." I passed that on.

When we found the soft shoulder, or verge as Sir Reginald

had called it, the mountain climbed higher to our right, before the road curved and descended back towards the east end of the valley.

Io had his phone out. "I sent the location to Owain. Fortunately the normal SatNav works here. Faerie GPS relies on the pixies, and they don't always mark things as well as they should." He glanced around, then shrugged. "Would you ask Sir Reginald if he'd like a look under my bonnet?"

"You don't have a hat on..."

"The car," Io said and pulled the lever. The hood of the car popped.

"Most definitely," Sir Reginald said from the back seat and darted out through the windshield... or windscreen. All of these new British terms made my head ache.

"Looks like a normal engine," I said once I was out. I left a gap between me and Io. A Sir-Reginald-sized gap.

Io pulled his wand out of his sleeve and tapped the engine with it. The heat rising off the metal swirled and faded away. A large metal, ceramic, and who knows what else tank was there. Hoses and pipes ran off the large... whatever it was. There was the odour of something burning. Coal and sulphur stung my nose.

"A lot of potential in there," Sir Reginald said. "If he gets a demon upgrade, he could race with the top cars."

"That's my goal," Io said once I repeated the comments. "I put my money into getting the car built, not into the demon. I only had enough funds this year to purchase a level two."

"Wait," I interjected. "You're talking like there's a real demonic critter in that tank."

"There is," Io and Sir Reginald said together.

"The tank binds them into place." Io pointed to something next to the large tank. "Through that port, we feed them magical energy, and they convert it into speed and power."

"What do you feed them for power?" I took a step back, not sure what a demon would want to eat.

"Magic mushrooms, enchanted glow rocks, or in a pinch, I can give it a blast with my wand. That, however, takes energy from me."

"Several drivers on the top fae circuit were banned a few decades ago for locking pixies in their intake tanks," Sir Reginald added. "The demons sucked the pixies dry of power whenever a dash of speed was needed."

"Like a tank of nitrous oxide," Jake added. He explained what nitrous was and how it affected an internal combustion engine. I caught Io up on the ghostly conversation.

"So," I said, a sly smile tweaking my mouth, "this is really an infernal combustion engine?"

"Indeed," Io said and pointed to a metal plate attached to the big tank. "Their best model, short of what they build for the Royal Marines."

"Oh." I was proud of my pun. And turned out it was a real term.

"Sir Reginald and I are going down to his wreck," Jake said.

"Please stay here, Miss Dymestl." Sir Reginald waved towards the slope. "As I said, what is left of me down there is not a pretty sight for a lady."

"Perhaps some wand training?" I looked at Io. "The ghosts are going into the valley. Can you give me a lesson while we wait?"

By the time Inspector Owain pulled his squad car in behind Io's Mini, I was getting the hang of poking my wand into my sleeve or the waistband of my skirt. A little surge of magic from me and it went... somewhere.

"It's still there, but it's not," Io said when I asked.

"How? Where? Can you be more specific?"

"Because magic?" He shrugged.

Behind the inspector, a tow truck barely wedged itself off the road. It was huge compared to Io's shiny blue Mini. The doors opened and half a dozen short, stocky humans piled out of the truck. Well, almost humans. Fae of some sort, due to their pointy ears. They all had long narrow beards and fluffy eyebrows to go with their ears. Each wore a dark-blue jacket and matching trousers. Embroidery on the back of the jacket read "Gnarly Recovery. If we can't get it unstuck, you don't want to recover it."

"Gnarly!" I said and laughed.

"Ga-narly, miss," the eldest of the gnomes said. His voice was high pitched but not as shrill as those of the pixies. "Family name. All of us pronounce the G."

"Ebrel Dymestl," Owain said, "daughter of Jasmine, niece of Rhosyn, this is Gnorm Gnarly." He pronounced each G in the gnome's name as a hard sound.

"Honoured, Miss Dymestl. You've got quite the family pedigree. Well respected and honourable."

"Thank you. A pleasure to meet you as well," I said. "Pardon my asking, please. Are you a gnome?"

"Ga-nome," he said with a chuckle. "Americans always have problems remembering to add the ga sound to our names."

A male pixie darted up and hovered between Owain and Gnorm. Even the small fae had a Gnarly jacket on, though with slits where his wings flittered out.

"We got big trouble, bosses," he squeaked.

"What?" they both said.

"The containment cauldron cracked on that wreck," the pixie said, hovering between the officer and the gnome. "It's been oozing. Ichor and now little demonettes. They're pulling at the crack, trying to make it wide enough for the big guy to escape."

"How big is big?" Owain asked.

The pixie shrugged. "The car is too mangled to see the info plate with the rating."

"I'm afraid," Sir Reginald said, popping in next to me, "it's a beefy 4.6 experimental demon."

I shared that.

Gnorm whistled.

"We don't have a containment vessel large enough to hold that," he said. "All the racers are full up, prepped out for the new fae road season."

"What if we call the Royal Marines?" Owain asked. "The last time we had a demon get loose, MI-13 was very displeased. Her Royal Majesty even sent a pixie dispatch. That was one loud pixie."

"I remember," Gnorm said. "That's why we added level-four containment to all our trucks. But a 4.6 is too big for even that. Only the pro-circuit racers get those. Who is this gent we're pulling out of the ravine?"

"There wasn't enough of him left to know," the pixie said and shrugged.

"You didn't tell him?" I asked.

"We didn't want word getting out," Jones said. "Too many mundanes could overhear. We never know who's on the other end of a call. Sir Reginald Dewsberry," he told the gnome.

"I heard they gave him a permit for an experimental racing demon in his personal car. Figured he'd run off to the continent to live the anonymous life."

Another pixie in a Gnarly jacket zipped towards us.

"Boss, we need to get on this!" it yelled. "The cauldron is about to split. That demon is almost out, and it will be huge."

Owain glanced at me, worry leaking through his tough-cop expression. He jerked his phone out of his pocket.

"Rhosyn," he said after he hit the display. "We've got a demon. Big one. I need you."

8

Io nudged me. He had his own wand in hand.

"This isn't the lesson I had planned," he said and nodded towards my waist. I put my hand on my skirt's waistband and sent the little surge of magic that retrieved my wand from wherever it went.

"Did I hear correctly," Io asked, "that you've got a 4.6 demon about to get loose?"

"Probably down to a 4.5 now that it oozed off some demonettes," Owain said. "I haven't seen one that large since I worked with Rose down in Australia before the Great War."

"My Mini has an Infernal containment device rated for 4.5. It only has a 2.3 in it now."

Owain looked up from his phone when I told them. He and Gnorm exchanged a long look, then each nodded.

"Risky, but worth a go."

"I'll get my lads pulling your demon into our containment cauldron," Gnorm said. The gnomes shifted from setting up their winches to pulling metallic hoses from the back of their wrecker.

"Ebrel, dearie," Aunt Rose said next to me.

I jumped.

"How did you get here so fast?"

"Magic, my dear." She wore her spectacles, but they had a bluish tint to them. "We'll teach you, perhaps in twenty or thirty years. Transportation spells are rather advanced, and you just got your wand yesterday."

Punkin rubbed against me.

"You too? How come everyone can do the magical travel bit except me?

"I hitched a ride," Punkin said. "You're new, so don't expect to be popping off to fetch a pint in the evening. You'll need a good fifty years or so to learn."

"That's why I've got a familiar, right?" I reached down and scruffed his head behind his ears. "You're far more catlike than I imagined a house elf would be."

"Pwca, please!" he said. "A century as a cat has taught me that felines run the human world. You'll scratch my cheeks whenever I want."

"Yeah, right," I said, then jerked my hand away from his fuzzy face.

"You can't resist," he said smugly.

Owain filled Aunt Rose in on the situation. Io and I watched the gnomes work to hook a hose up, bridging his Mini and the wrecker. One gnome grunted and locked the hose into Io's cauldron. A wave of sulphur stench hit me.

"Brimstone," Io said. "The demon's not happy. He likes the room in there." The sound of a pump, like a vacuum, started. Growling intensified, and a bulge grew in the end of the hose. A demon-shaped bulge. At least, it was what I thought a demon might look like. Kind of like a large bulldog with horns and spikes.

"I thought you said it was huge?" That bulge in the hose

wasn't as large as Io had led me to believe. "Will it rip through that hose?"

"Don't be worrying, lass," the gnome foreman said. "The hoses knock them to about a quarter of their normal size."

"You mean that thing is four times as large as it looks?" I winced. It wouldn't be pretty or nice if the hose split.

"Gnorm had us shift a 3.7 just last week. We refreshed the containment spells on the hose right after to make sure we'd handle anything up to a four."

"Is that what you're planning to do with the demon down there?" I asked Owain. "Run a hose down and bring it up here?"

"Unfortunately, no," the inspector said. "Gnorm's men are layering on temporary binding spells. They won't hold a beast that large for long. Once the Bobbies arrive, we'll cut the binding spells on Sir Reginald's cauldron. If it doesn't break free first."

"Won't the demon escape?" I asked, wrapping my arms around my chest. After seeing the shape of what they were pulling from Io's car, I didn't want to meet its big brother.

"We have to, or call in the Royal Marines," Owain said. "And that means a visit to MI-13."

"Which is?"

"Like the CIA, but dealing with magic and fae," Owain said. He had gone pale. "They really, really don't like to fill out the paperwork for demonic episodes. The last time one broke loose up in Edinburgh, the Queen called the agent overseeing the operation to a private audience."

"A royal scolding," Io said. Even he had gone pale at the notion.

"So far I've avoided being dressed down by Her Royal Majesty. I'd like to keep it that way."

"Then let's make sure we do this one right," Aunt Rose said. "Good, the Bobbies are here."

A dark lorry arrived and blocked the road. Looked more like a SWAT vehicle or special ops van from the movies. All black, with thick steel and thick, heavy greenish windows.

"A bunch of cops are going to take on a demon?" I shook my head.

"Not just cops," Owain said. "Bobbies. You'll see in a moment."

All I could picture was the archetypical British bobby with his domed hat, twirling his club.

"Just wait," Rose said.

The back of the truck opened, and out swarmed a multitude of... well, they looked like upright green-skinned, feral boars. Beefy man-shaped figures with tusks and flat noses. If it weren't for their heads, they'd look great on any body-building advert. All wore dark military-style vests, goggles, and had long clubs that sparked with green or blue magic.

"Orcs?"

"Bobbies, miss," the lead one said. "Robert 34-764 at your service, Inspector." He locked his gaze with Aunt Rose. "I didn't realise it was serious enough to call you in."

"A 4.6 experimental model. Down in the ravine. Containment cauldron about to split wide open and let it loose," Aunt Rose said. "Your Bobbies should push it to this ridge. Owain and I will take care of the containment."

"Why does everyone think my sweet aunt Rose is a big bad demon hunter?" I whispered to Io.

"Because she is a big bad demon hunter," Io said. "She trained all the Australians. They've got the biggest demon portal. She tired of living down there. Wanted to retire back to Britain."

"Right. Lads, get the wires set." Robert 34-whatever-he-was pointed towards where the pixies were darting back and forth. He turned to Aunt Rose. "What do you want us to do?"

"Drive it up here," she said. "We'll contain it in the Mini's cauldron."

"What's its rating?"

"Four point five, by Infernal," Io said. "Newest model."

"Oh, and don't worry about shaving off a few demonettes on the way," Owain said. "I'd rather not try to contain a full 4.6 in a 4.5 cauldron."

"Pesky little buggers," Robert the orc leader said. "Robert 629!" he said into the radio mic on his lapel. "Give me a time estimate on how long that broken cauldron can hold together."

"Three, maybe four minutes, tops," the radio crackled.

"Are they all named Robert?"

"All orcs are," Punkin said. "Makes it easier, or so they say. That's why we call them the Bobbies."

"Robert 784," Robert the leader said, keying his mic again. "If it pops before I get down there, drive the entity up the ravine towards containment."

"Cauldron on the car has failed," the radio said. "Demon has escaped. Repeat, demon has escaped the car's containment. Blimey, that beast is huge, Captain 34-764."

"Clip its toenails on the way up," Robert said. "You lads have your mini-containers ready?"

"Three-twenty-niner, here. Demonette containment crew standing by."

"Roger that," the Bobby captain responded. "Expect a plethora of the little buggers. We need to knock this one down a size or two."

"Copy that!"

"I'll leave the capture of the big beastie to the professionals," the Robert captain said and included Io and I in his sweeping gaze. "I will go assist my crew and keep it headed your way." He turned and jogged down the steep incline.

"We're the professional demon catchers?"

9

My wand was still in my hand.

"Leave my familiar alone!" I growled. The pent-up adrenaline in me surged. I released it through the wand. A dark-emerald bolt of magic shot out. The demon jerked its paw back and yipped. A demonette popped off him.

"Again, Ebrel," Aunt Rose called.

I was on my knees and aimed my wand around the car, holding with both hands like I was on a police show back in the States. The demon focused on me. He swiped long talons my way. Owain shot another blast into his side, driving it back. The paw raked Io's car, leaving long scratches in the paint.

"Don't hurt Io's car, either." I unleashed another bolt at the beast. Trapped against the rock wall, I had nowhere to run, so my fight-or-flight was all fight. This time the emerald blast knocked the demon back. Two dog-sized demonettes popped off it. More Bobbies were on them in a flash. The big beast tumbled back under my blast, right into Aunt Rose's ruby-pink ray. The magic of her wand spread around the beast, shrinking it as she pushed it towards Io's engine. The cauldron sucked the demon in through the funnel with a satisfying plop and gurgle into the car's containment cell.

Two gnomes charged out of the wrecker. One jerked the funnel-shaped port off the containment chamber. The other slammed a cap on the pipe and twisted it shut. He pulled a big wrench out of a little pocket on his trouser leg and clamped it onto the nub on the cap. Sparks flew, and a final belch of brimstone stung the air. Both gnomes used their sleeves to wipe their brows and high-fived each other.

Io's car jerked once. It a gave a burp, shook, made a small rattle, then settled down.

"Probably about a 4.4 now, Miss Dymestl," Sir Reginald said. "You're good with that wand."

"Nice shooting, Tex," Jake said. "I knew you had some southwest in you."

I ignored him and fought the urge to shake. I had just faced down a demon. A flippin' DEMON!

Aunt Rose leaned on the fender of the Mini. She wiped the sweat off her brow again. After a moment, she was back to being her demure, prim and proper Welsh grand-aunt, not a magic-slinging demon hunter. She looked at Owain, then at me.

"Very good, dearie," she said and slid her wand back into her sleeve, then wiped her hands on her apron. I halfway expected her to pull a plate of biscuits and a cuppa out of her sleeve.

"How high did she score on the crystals?" Owain asked.

"Nine sixty-seven," Io said. "I had to collect them all and do the tally."

"Are you okay?" I asked. His clothing was dirty, and he had a tear down one of his sleeves. He patted himself, then grinned.

"I had time to put a cushion spell behind me. Racing has given me fast reflexes." His eye caught the tear in his shirt. Io ran the glowing tip of his wand down it. The fabric mended itself in the green light.

"Wait a moment," I said. "You indicated only two other witches scored higher than I did on the crystals test. What does that measure?"

"Raw magic power," Owain said. "Both the strength and the various types. The test is fairly comprehensive in measuring potential." He glanced at Aunt Rose. "You didn't tell her?"

"She's only been here two days."

"Tell me what? Who scored higher than me? And what does it mean, raw magic power?"

"The two who scored highest on the crystals, ever," Owain said, "are the two sisters."

"Two sisters... Who are?"

"Her grace, Queen of the Fae, and Rhosyn."

I shot Aunt Rose a glare. "You could have told me you were some super-powerful witch."

"Would you have believed me if I told you when I invited to you come to the valley?"

I still wasn't inclined to believe my Auntie Rose, with her prim and proper British grandma appearance, was a powerful witch. "No... well, I would have thought you were crazy."

"And not come at all," Aunt Rose said. "We needed to get you to the valley first."

"I've been here two days already." I felt miffed that they had kept me in the dark about something so important.

"You're a tad beastly in the morning," Punkin said. He crawled out from under the Mini and jumped on the hood—on the bonnet. "Then you go scampering off to climb rocks and be alone."

This time I stuck my tongue out at him. Punkin was right. I hadn't been the most sociable person. Jet lag. And a new environment.

"Sorry. What did those crystals tell about me?"

"The crystals measure the amount of power of different

types of magic one can wield," Aunt Rose said. "Owain scored high in magical force and intuitiveness. He's good at solving magical puzzles and at slamming monsters around. That's why he makes a good demon catcher."

"I scored highest in dexterity types of magic, and in illusions," Io said. "I make a great artist, and I hope, a great racer with this new demon."

"What did these crystals say about me?" I looked at Aunt Rose.

"You scored high in all areas."

"And that means?"

She was quiet under my gaze, but returned it, not breaking eye contact.

Punkin rubbed against my legs.

"It means once you've been trained," he said, "maybe a decade or two, you can undo the curse Her Grace put on me, and give me my old form back."

"Fat chance, Fuzzbutt," I said. "Even I know not go against a queen. Especially one I'm related to."

Then it hit me. I sagged back against the Mini. "Does that mean I'm some sort of princess or something?"

"Technically, you do have titles, dearie," said Aunt Rose. "But my sister has several daughters already. We're far down the line of succession for her throne."

"That's one small good thing today," I said. "I have no desire to be a princess. Just a barista."

"Hey! You saved my fuzzy bum," Punkin said. "I'd call that a good thing."

"We'll see if I was right in that decision," I said.

Owain chuckled. The first time I'd seen a crack in his cop demeanour.

"And a witch," Aunt Rose said. "You're a Dymestl, and we're chuffed about that."

"Heya! Inspector!" Gnorm called. He peered over the edge of the ravine. "You should come down and see the car's demon containment system."

"Because it has a size-4.6-demon-sized crack in it?"

"No," the gnome said. "Because there are some very tiny holes in the cauldron block. Someone wanted that demon to escape."

Something started bugging me. I decided to just ask.

"What about Sir Reginald?" I looked at Aunt Rose for the answer. "He was fae and a cricket player. Did he use magic to make himself better?"

"That wouldn't have been cricket," Aunt Rose said.

"I understand your question," Sir Reginald said. "For one outside of our culture, one who has had no exposure to the true sport of gentlemen, it's an understandable question. And the answer is no. As your aunt said, that would violate the spirit of the game. No magic in cricket, ever."

"What did he say, dearie?" Aunt Rose, with her magic spectacles perched on her nose, looked towards Sir Reginald.

"He said it wouldn't be cricket, just like you said."

"And to make sure," she added, "the queen herself crafted special amulets for all fae players to wear. Anytime a fae was on the pitch, there was a fae referee there to oversee the game. We British, even the fae British, take our cricket very seriously."

Jake floated next to Sir Reginald. "Like a blackjack player counting cards," he said. "That's cheating, even if it's a natural ability."

Owain returned several moments later.

"Definitely sabotage," he said with a glance at Aunt Rose. "Someone wanted that demon to get out."

"What makes you think that?"

"I could see the holes in the cauldron's spell shield. Tiny pinpricks. They're just big enough and just close enough to eventually cause a rupture in the containment spells. It's a wonder the impact of the initial crash didn't split it wide open."

"Who had the knowledge to do such a thing?" I asked.

"Most of the racing mechanics," he said, donning his own set of goggles. They looked like a set of antique optometrist examination lenses attached to a leather strap by a series of rods. One of about twenty lenses could be lowered over each eye. Owain lowered one set after another until he nodded at the sight of Sir Reginald and Jake.

"Who was your auto designer?"

"Kerry Kentwhistle," Sir Reginald said. "Indisputable reputation. The best at his art." I translated again.

"And he got you the 4.6?"

Sir Reginald blushed and stared at where his feet would have been, if he had a fully formed body.

"I sourced it myself," Sir Reginald said. "I passed along all the paperwork to make sure I had the proper specification. Kentwhistle always enchants his racing cauldrons right to the edge, but short of the military-grade specifications. That demon shouldn't have escaped even in a crash that bad."

Owain listened to my translation and nodded. "He's got the best reputation in the cauldron business. The Infernal company uses his spell designs in all of their cauldrons." He bit his lower lip and looked back at Aunt Rose. She shrugged.

"Where did you find the demon?"

"One of my contacts in the cricket world turned me on to a source," Sir Reginald said.

"Who?"

"Bryce Rustle."

"The star Australian batter?"

"Yes," Sir Reginald said. "He's also a racer and said his fellows down under had a portal that kept spitting out demons almost at a military grade. It took some doing, but I got the stamps and approvals from MI-13 to import one. They had it held up in magical customs for over a year. That's why I played a season longer than I had indicated. I needed something to do to keep from going down to the port every week to pester the clerks holding my racing engine."

"Her Royal Majesty would be very irate if an almost-military-grade Australian demon rampaged across the Welsh country-side," Aunt Rose said.

🜋 10 🜋

I got to ride in the front of Owain's police cruiser to Castle Raven. Io and Aunt Rose headed back to Mystic Brews. I wasn't sure what kind of damage Nia and her sister Mia could do to our café running tea time by themselves.

Owain wanted to interview the Earl and Lady Edeirnion while both I and Sir Reginald were available. Punkin sat in the back, darting from window to window, not aware he was running through the ghostly bodies of Jake and Sir Reginald.

"Do you have a demon in this thing, too?"

"Of course, though it's the only one in our constabulary motor pool."

"Why is that?"

"I'm the only fae on the force in this area. Got several up in Gwynedd, and more down in Cardiff. Where more mundanes interact with fae, more fae constables are needed."

"No wonder Aunt Rose wants to bring more tourists into Misty Valley," I said. "The rest of Wales is getting all the tourists."

"I hope we've waited long enough for the earl to rise."

"Nobles have issues with waking before sundown? Sounds like he's quite the partier."

"He's a vamp, as is Lady Edeirnion," Owain said, navigating the twisting and turning road up the mountain. An imposing structure stood at the top of the road. One that made me think of old Christopher Lee movies.

"You don't mean he's a real vampire, right?"

"Of course. I keep forgetting that you weren't raised as part of the fae."

"My mom and dad divorced when I was three. Dad said she was crazy, always listening to voices. So the judge gave him custody of me."

"She could hear ghosts," Owain said. "That was her only magic power beyond a few minor spells and effects. Once word spreads that you have her same gift, you'll probably not have a moment's peace."

"Oh, great!"

"Don't worry, Miss Dymestl," Sir Reginald said. "We in the ghostly enclaves have spread word that you are to be bothered only in the direst of circumstances. We learned from what your mother went through. The fae queen has issued an edict that only emergency contact be made with you. The edict came too late with your mother's case. She'd already withdrawn from fae society."

"And I'm here to watch your back," Jake said.

"You've got my back?" I turned to look at him.

"Of course," both Jake and Punkin said.

"Not you, Fuzzbutt, I was talking to Jake."

"You saved my bum, that means you like me," Punkin said. "So I've got your back."

"Thanks Fuzzbutt, I'll remember that."

"Please, not Fuzzbutt!" Punkin shot me a glare.

"Punk, then."

"That's worse. Do you give nicknames to all your familiars?"

"You're my first familiar, Fuzzbutt," I said. "And yes, all my pets had nicknames."

"I'm not a pet."

"You look like one," I said. "What do familiars do?"

"Not much," he said. "You witches give us treats and scritches and piles of coffee grounds to chew on."

"That's right. You're addicted to coffee grounds," I said, squinting. "I'll be chatting with Aunt Rose about keeping you out of my dump bins."

"A familiar is there to help enhance your magic," Owain said. "Unfortunately, you become responsible for their actions. Keep an eye on that one. I'd hate to have to charge you with aiding and abetting because he did one of his usual tricks."

"What have I gotten into?" I slumped down in my seat.

"I'll help watch him," Jake said.

"You both need watching," I responded.

Owain slowed his car and rolled to a stop by the ornate iron gates that blocked the road up to the castle... or manor... or whatever that building was. He pulled a silver wand out of his sleeve and tapped a pad on the pedestal next to the car.

"One moment, Inspector Owain," a voice crackled out of a hidden speaker in the pedestal. "I shall alert Earl and Lady Edeirnion to your arrival."

With that, the gates swung open. I caught another whiff of brimstone as the engine growled to climb the steep road.

"Wow! My first castle," I said as we climbed out. Jake and Sir Reginald just slid through the doors again. Punkin jumped out and stayed by my side.

"Fortified manor house, actually," Owain said. "Though we call it Castle Raven. Helps with the tourism if they believe we have a real castle."

I shrugged. The walls were stone. The main door, a heavy

wooden one banded with iron, swung open. Looked like a castle to my American eyes.

A man in a nice suit and an ascot instead of a tie waved us in.

"Welcome to Caer Cigfran. The Earl and Lady are in the Earl's study, last door to the right, Inspector."

"Many thanks, Jonathan," Owain said.

The man glanced down at Punkin, who was sitting and licking his front paw, then up at me.

"A pleasure to meet you, Lady Ebrel," he said with a bow. "Would your familiar care for a dish of milk?"

"A large cappuccino," Punkin said. "Dash of vanilla powder on top."

The man bowed as though a talking cat were nothing new. Owain started towards the far end of the hallway.

"Seriously? That's what you like?" I whispered, afraid my voice would carry in the dark and vast cavern of the stone and timber hall.

"I don't know," Punkin said. "He looked like he needed something to do, so I ordered what one of the tourists requested today."

"Inspector," a deep voice called as we entered the double doors into another dark hall. "What brings you to our humble abode?"

"I'd call this anything but humble," Punkin said.

"Ah, Lady Ebrel," the man said. He was dressed in dark trousers, with a blood-red jacket over a button-front shirt. The jacket looked like it belonged on the set of a Sherlock Holmes BBC show. A smoking jacket, if I remembered correctly. "So good to meet you. Please, may I offer you and the inspector refreshments? We have wine, ale, and coffee. I can ring for a fizzy drink if you prefer."

"Oh, whatever you're having is fine."

A feminine chuckle rang out. A woman in a long dress of

deep green glided into view. This was a dark cavern of a room. Didn't they believe in windows or lights?

"Please forgive our lack of windows," she said. "We had them removed from most of the house centuries ago. Daylight doesn't agree with us. As for the beverage, what we're having won't suit your tastes, nor your constitution, my dear."

She extended her hand.

"Lady Edeirnion. There, I've been all formal. Please call me Rhian, and we'll pretend that all the nobility rules of etiquette have been applied." Just like Aunt Rhosyn's name, the guttural Hr sound was at beginning of Rhian's name.

She waved towards a set of comfortable-looking leather chairs near a fireplace. A log burned in the fireplace, with no smell of smoke. I thought of the lesson Io had given me and reached out with my fledgling magic senses. The fire glowed with the sense of a spell in play.

Owain led us towards the chairs and waved me towards one. The earl gestured as well.

"Please sit. Do you prefer wine or coffee?" He and his wife each glided into chairs near the fire. They were turned to face back into the vast room. Nearly empty wine goblets sat on small tables at their elbows.

The butler, or servant, or whatever he was, sat a bowl on a saucer on the floor next to me.

"Cappuccino with a dash of vanilla powder for your familiar," he said. "And I took the liberty of contacting Miss Nia at the café. She said you prefer something I believe is a caramel macchiato." He handed me a tall ceramic mug, topped with whipped cream and caramel sauce.

"That's Nia's favourite," I said. "But I enjoy them too."

Jonathan retrieved a bottle from a champagne bucket near the fire. No sweat from an ice bath graced the ornate bucket. He poured into the glasses of the earl and lady. Thick dark-amber liquid streamed forth.

"What region?" I asked, trying to see the label on the bottle. "My father has been trying to get me to learn wine."

Rhian smiled.

"I doubt he follows our varietals," she said.

"Blood," Owain said.

I closed my mouth, realising I was staring at the cup in Rhian's hands. She raised it to her lips. Pointed fangs glistened in the firelight.

"You really are vampires," I whispered.

"I did tell you," Owain said.

"Did you have anything to do"—the earl waved his glass towards the outside wall—"with the commotion in the ravine this afternoon?"

"Whatever was all of that?" Rhian asked. "I felt several magical surges, and Jonathan got a glimpse of the Bobby van on the mountain road.

"That was Ebrel, Rhosyn, Io, and I," Owain said. "We had an almost military-grade demon on the loose."

The earl whistled. "The Australians have been getting bigger ones out of their portal. I'll have a talk with Bryce Rustle when he arrives for the commission meeting in a few days."

"Ebrel just received her wand, according to the Mystic Mystery," Rhian said. "And you took her to hunt down a military-level demon?"

"Rhosyn was with me," Owain said, squirming in his chair. He had a cup of tea in his hand and rotated it on his saucer to discharge his nervous energy.

"I did pretty good for my second day," I said. "Two of those pit-bull-sized demonettes popped off when I blasted it."

"Oh, good show, my dear," Rhian said, then turned her steely gaze back on Owain.

"It didn't start out as a demon hunt," he said and tried to put his cop face back on. It didn't stay. He squirmed like a child caught dipping into the candy before meal time. "Unfortunately we were there to close the case on a missing person."

"Not Reg?" the earl asked.

Owain nodded and reached into his inner jacket. I sensed a little surge of magic, like when I pulled my wand out of its storage place. He summoned his headband with all the optometrist lenses again.

"Where is he, Ebrel?"

I pointed towards an empty chair between myself and Earl Edeirnion.

"Oh, welcome, Sir Reginald," the earl said. His eyes slid past the spirit, not seeing him.

"Please tell Macsen and Rhian I most appreciate their hospitality," Sir Reginald said. "I profusely apologise for putting their soiree to disgrace by driving off that cliff."

I translated, trying to stay in third person, and started stumbling over titles.

"I'm Macsen," the earl said.

"As I said, please, call me Rhian, dear. I understand how difficult following all of these titles can be, especially for you young Americans."

"You're practically family," Macsen added. "Rhosyn is one of our dearest friends. Being her niece and Jasmine's daughter will open many doors for you. Your family is well respected."

"I just want to run my coffee bar," I said.

"If we can get back to the night of your party for Sir Reginald," Owain interjected.

"Of course," Rhian said. "What was it, dear, close to two hundred guests that night?"

"I believe Jonathan has the official list saved on his tablet or whatever those things are called."

"You'd still be using quills and scrolls if I let you, dear," Rhian said.

"Was there anyone who seemed off that night?" Owain interjected.

"Off? Like how?" Macsen asked.

"Seemed insulted, miffed, or had a grudge about Sir Reginald for any reason?"

"Those were my fellow cricket men and women," Sir Reginald said with a tone of irritation. "It wouldn't be cricket to hold a grudge."

I translated that. Rhian shook her head. Macsen rubbed his long drooping moustache.

"Yerdleh was miffed. But he always is."

"Ah, yes." Sir Reginald sighed. "I'd forgotten about him."

"You mean the mayor?" These names were confusing, however, I thought I remembered that one.

"Yes, he was quite put off by his treatment that season, and he announced his retirement," Macsen said. "Several years before Reg retired."

"He's still carrying the grudge about the Dewsberry spinner?" Owain asked.

"Not just the bowling. He still feels insulted that Sir Reginald didn't give him a chance to hit it again that game."

"Poor fellow was so put off by the new pitch that I tried to help him with a regular pitch the next time he was at the wickets." Sir Reginald sounded so contrite, I stifled a giggle.

"Did he tell you he bowled regular pitches to Yerdleh the rest of the match?" Macsen chuckled. "The fellow refused to move his bat for anything except the Dewsberry spinner after that. His team captain benched him for the season."

"He was out of the running for the Spirit of Cricket Award that year," Owain said.

"Yerdleh was never in the running for it," Macsen added.

"Still, it was a pity he was on the English team when our Reginald was bowling for the Welsh team. Yerdleh is a good batter against fastballs, but little else."

"Had their other top batsman not taken ill that week, Yerdleh wouldn't have been pressed into bat against Reg. The captains shouldn't have put him against a spin bowler."

"Yerdleh returned here to Misty Valley," Rhian added for my benefit. "He's English on his father's side and fae from our valley on his mother's. The old mayor retired. A century and a half in office were enough for him. Yerdleh jumped at the chance to get the prestige of the office." Rhian took another sip of her red liquid.

I gave a slight shudder.

"My dear," she said, "we only import synthetic now. I love the French varietals from this season."

"So, people don't actually bleed into those bottles?"

"Of course not." Her fangs showed when she smiled. "The fae at the blood farms only need a few drops of real blood, then they can replicate it with spells. The true art is in mixing it across species and families. They won't share which families. Our favourite mixes pixie, troll, and human blood. Stout and full bodied, with a zing to it."

"That's the pixie end of the spectrum," Macsen added. "You were about to add, dear?"

"You asked if anyone was off," Rhian said. "We did have that intruder once Sir Reginald had left."

"Oh, yes. His housekeeper."

"Seonag?" Sir Reginald exclaimed. "Whatever was she doing here?"

"You had an intruder?" Owain asked, raising his spectre goggles. "Did you notify us?"

"There was no need," Macsen said.

"Elain found her a short while after Reg left." I was still getting used to Welsh names. Rhian pronounced each letter in a rolling lilt, eh-lah-in. She grabbed an electronic table and flipped open its case. "I'll text her to see if she can come down."

"Why was Seonag here?" Sir Reginald asked again. "She had said she was staying at my manor that evening."

I passed that on.

"How long has she been in your employ?" Owain asked.

"About a decade," Sir Reginald said. "Mother doesn't seem fond of her. She has gone off on how I shouldn't have employed a Scotswoman here in Wales."

"Was your mother prejudiced?" I asked. Owain kept writing to get my translation down.

"Remember, I hardly knew her before I died," Sir Reginald said. "Mother and Father had a fiery marriage, and they finally had an argument that blew up several blocks of Swansea. I'm told that MI-13 had quite the time erasing memories and photos of the altercation and its aftermath."

"I remember that," Macsen said.

"MI-13 called in every constable for support and evidence erasure. Mobile phones weren't around yet, nor the internet. The few reports of activity that got out were latched on to by the Irish dissidents. They took responsibility without being asked."

"There wasn't much left of Mr Dewsberry, and nothing of Sir Reginald's mother." Owain nodded towards the chair where the ghost sat. "Pass my apologies on to Sir Reginald."

"Quite all right, Inspector," he replied. "I went to live with Lieutenant Colonel Reece. An admirable man." I passed that on, even saying it as he did: "Leftenant Colonel."

"Old Rhodri," Macsen said for my benefit. "Excellent chap. Good fae lineage in his family. Pity his wife died in the blast between the Dewsberrys."

"Rhodri said that's why he took me in," Sir Reginald said. "He wanted to make a positive out of a tragedy. An excellent role model. A man of firm character. He even tooled around with my father on several missions for the predecessor of MI-13."

"The Queen's Service until the Great War," Macsen said. "That's when it officially shifted to the new designation. Wasn't Rhodri also part of that raid on the rakshasa demon?"

"I believe so," Sir Reginald said. "He was full of stories about his time in service. Still has his old elephant musket. He keeps it ready with depleted demonic shot."

"Look at me!" Jake came sailing across the room. The high ceilings of the great hall we were in had given him room to play. "Let me try superhero pose." He twisted so he was on his belly, arms outstretched. Owain chuckled.

"The spirit of my old boyfriend," I explained. "He is rather taken with the high ceilings here." Then I explained who he was and how he was zooming about their large room. My description of a feather-covered biker ghost brought a smile to Rhian's face.

A single chicken feather wafted down and landed on Macsen's smoking jacket. He plucked it off with a grin.

"Yours, I believe." He handed it to me. "Although feathers appearing from nowhere is something I'd expect from our lieutenant colonel."

"If I may ask," I ventured, "why is lieutenant pronounced differently here? In America we say 'loo-tenant'?"

"A bit of anti-Norman sentiment, I'm afraid," Macsen said. "The Normans were the French invaders from back around the ninth and tenth centuries. We Britons, especially those of us from the Welsh side of our island, didn't think fondly of them. I was among those. The Norman invaders kept calling and knocking down my fort. Every time I'd rebuild it, they'd come back half a century later and try to dismantle it and anyone in it."

"You can share your stories about the old times later, milord," Rhian said, then turned toward me. "We anglicized the pronunciation of lieutenant. I believe Rhodri served in the brief time we rebelled enough to change the spelling to how it is pronounced. It's editors, my dear, and grammarians, who seem more worried about spellings than how the word is pronounced."

"You needed me, Mother?" another feminine voice said from the doorway.

A woman, thin and tall with mocha skin, entered. Confident, her chin raised, back straight. Dark slacks and blouse, either navy or black, under a long cardigan of lighter grey graced her figure. She wore her dark hair long below shoulder length.

"Yes, Elain, Inspector Owain has a few questions—"

"April! Look out!" Something fluttered over me, towards the new woman.

I fell to the floor. Jake pointed behind me, to where the wet bar stood. Punkin looked up from his dish of cappuccino and licked the cream off his whiskers.

"What?"

Elain grabbed whatever fluttered, spun, and launched it at the bar. The sound of a knife embedding into the dark wood, followed by vibrating twang of metal, sounded in the hushed room.

"Children!" Rhian said. "Not when we have guests. And fix that slice in the wood before you leave, young man."

"Very well, Mother," a male voice said from the wet bar. "How did you hear?"

"I told you," Elain said. "You sharpen your blades on the false edge too far down."

The knife thrower came to join us, flipping a knife in his hand.

"Don't sit there, Neirin," she warned, pointing at the empty chair next to me. "Sir Reginald's spirit is with us today."

"Seriously?" Elain asked. Her eyes slid to me. "You must be Lady Ebrel." She held her hand out to help me to my feet.

"Thank you. Would you be Lady Elain? I'm still trying to learn all the thees and such."

"How about just Elain? I wanted to come down to Mystic Brews to meet you tomorrow morning."

"Aren't you like your parents?" My eyes slid to Rhian and Macsen, sipping their blood.

"A vamp? I'm not. Neirin and I are both adopted. Tell me you noticed the skin colour at least." She chuckled with the last part. "I hear from the pixies you make a mean macchiato. Do you mind if I come hang out in the mornings?"

"Please do." She was about my age, maybe. I was learning that appearances in the fae community were deceiving. Elain raised her hand towards her brother after releasing mine. Her brother took it and laid a gentle kiss on the back.

"He just tried to kill you?" I was confused.

"No, he tested me. We're a team, and we keep each other sharp with surprise."

"As often as you two attack each other in this house, I'm surprised it's still standing," Macsen said. "Neirin, Ebrel Dymestl, niece of Rhosyn. Thee and thou each other and call it finished so we can all be friends."

Neirin gave a stately bow, one leg extended and his arm out in a flourish.

"You grace our humble abode with your radiance, my lady," he said in a deep, rich tone. "I pray that you'll forgive my most unseemly interruption of your translation of my father's most esteemed deceased friend."

He reached out a hand towards me. I wasn't sure about him.

"Give him your hand, Ebrel," Rhian said. "Or he'll follow you around playing the love-struck and jilted fool."

"I am pleased to make your acquaintance, Lord Neirin," I said and laid my hand in his.

"I was knighted two centuries ago," he said. "My proper titles are—"

"Neirin," his mother said. "Stop trying to impress her. She's not your type."

"I don't even know what her blood type is?" He had another wine glass in hand and poured from the bottle between his parents.

"I'm confused," I interjected. "My apologies. Two days ago, I didn't even know fae existed, and now vampires? Who is which?"

"As you noted earlier," Elain said, "I'm not a vamp. Neirin is, though. He tried to get himself killed back during the Spanish Succession wars. Father was leading troops and didn't want him to die that night."

"He adopted me on the spot," Neirin said. "Which was good since the hole in my chest wasn't going to heal on its own."

I shut my eyes and rubbed my temples. This was getting to be too much.

"Perhaps the inspector can complete his investigation, and then you two can chat." Macsen raised his glass to punctuate his suggestion.

"You found an intruder the night of Sir Reginald's retirement party here?" Owain had his tablet on his lap, keyboard folded out, fingers hovering, ready to type.

"Yes," Elain said. "I was making a last sweep through the house. We tend to get stragglers who forget to go home. Some need to be carried out to the guest house to sleep it off, others just need a few more minutes with that special someone they're having fun with. I had all of them taken care of. Jonathan had the pwcas carry the last drunk off to bed."

"Where did you find the maid of Sir Reginald's?"

"Upstairs in the ballroom. We had a display set with some of his cricket memorabilia and his racing trophies."

"That is why we arranged Sir Reginald's memorabilia and trophies in the ballroom," Macsen added. "We had quite the time setting out all the plaques and awards. Jonathan had the pwcas going for a good day just on the racing awards, gloves, jumpsuit, and helmets."

"The entire display took us three entire nights to set out," Rhian said. "Fortunately, the lieutenant colonel was here to lend a keen eye. He's followed his foster son's careers and knows every single date on all the plaques and photos."

"I remember," Sir Reginald said. "I was fortunate that he didn't bring his elephant musket out. He's always been protective of me. Probably would have threatened to shoot anyone touching my cricket kit."

"What did the maid, this Seonag, say her purpose was?"

"She said she was trying to gather his equipment and take it back to his manor house."

"Such a thoughtful woman," Sir Reginald chimed in. "She was very meticulous in caring for everything in the home. Even my cars. She had places set for all of my cricket awards back in the manor house."

I passed that on. Owain kept typing.

"What did you do with Seonag?"

"After we woke the lieutenant colonel, he confirmed her identity and suggested that he'd cart off the materials by lorry in a week or so, once Sir Reginald returned home." Macsen waved towards his upper floor. "We've got them boxed, but Sir Reginald disappeared on us, so the lorry never came. The lieutenant colonel has been out of the country seeking him, convinced there is foul play about his disappearance."

"Have you informed the lieutenant colonel?" Rhian's tone was sombre.

"Not yet," Owain said. "Should make the call when I get back to the station."

"I would be honoured if you would make the call from here," Macsen said. "There's a fae line in my study. We could ring him together and support him as only military men can."

Owain closed his tablet and nodded.

"Sir Reginald." He lowered his spectacles again. "I'd suggest you remain here. This will be difficult enough on us."

"I understand, Inspector. My sincerest gratitude to both you and Macsen for taking care of my dearest friend."

W
e were so busy the at the end of our morning run that I wasn't even looking at the clients. Mia and Nia took care of the counter and getting the right cups and plates to them.

The last drink order of the shift waited for me.

"Caramel tornado!" I called out, reading the order. Both pixies wrote that on the orders instead of caramel macchiato. Nia was at my side as soon as I said it.

"Can you teach me again?" The woman who ordered was off to the side, her back to me. No one else was waiting, so I agreed.

"This one gets a single shot of espresso. Load the portafilter. Good, now use the tamper and press down on the grounds."

She was tentative and didn't go hard enough.

"One more time with more pressure. Pretend you're a troll."

"Grrr... Pay... Your... Toll!" Nia sang out as she stood on tiptoes to bear down on the tamper, but it worked. She got the steel down hard enough to pack the grounds in. They needed to be tight so the high-pressure water had to work to get through them.

"Good, now lock it in place." She twisted the round metal bowl of the portafilter into the machine. I walked her through the rest of the process. She wanted to put an extra scoop of caramel sauce in the cup. I had to remind her not to.

"Remember, not everyone is a pixie," I said. "We won't make any money if you give everyone free scoops."

"Oh! Real caramel? Not the flavoured syrup? Can you put extra in mine, please?" Elain said.

"Oh, hi! Sure, we'll give you an extra on the house," I said.

Nia shot me a glare. I shrugged. Six extra scoops for pixies a day or one for my newest friend. I knew how to do the math on that equation.

Elain again wore black with a deep-red cable-knit cardigan belted around her waist.

Nia stared at the spouts where the espresso came through the portafilter. Her eyes widened when the first stream appeared.

"How's the milk temp?" I asked.

"Right at the arrow you showed me on the dial."

"Good, pour them into the mug. Add the whipped cream to the top, and then the caramel drizzle."

Nia loved doing the drizzle. She moved the squeeze bottle around so the caramel made some strange design.

"It's a butterfly! Good?" Well, it kind of looked like an insect of some sort.

"Good," I said. "Tomorrow, I'll watch you make some for your pixie friends. If you do well, I'll teach you how to make a mocha."

"Really? A mocha!" Nia and Mia both gave excited squeals. "Wait until I tell our friends."

Elain giggled.

I glanced at the clock. Two minutes until the spell on the door locked it and the window shades went down.

"Grab a table," I told Elain. "I'll be out once I wipe down the station."

I gave the machine a quick flush and wipe down, then grabbed a cup of Kona and joined Elain.

"Pixies understand coffee?" she asked.

"Not really. This is only my third day even knowing that pixies exist," I said. The café had a few regular fae still inside. Aunt Rose said spells in the café urged only the humans to leave before the door locked. "I enjoy being with the pixies," I said, then shook my head. "There are several types of foo-foo coffee drinkers in the world. They break down into two main categories. Those who like syrupy milk drinks with some espresso in them."

"Like the pixies," Elain said. "And?"

"Espresso lovers," I said. "Once I get Nia trained to take care of the first kind, I want to work on attracting the second kind."

"Oh! Like an Italian espresso? Those were marvellous. If you need to do a research trip back to Milan, I'll go with!"

"I spent all of my annual trust payout getting this place set up with that coffee bar. A trip to Italy will have to wait."

Elain raised her cup for another sip and looked at me across the cup.

"Well, I'll be your travel partner," she said. She glanced around the café once, then spoke quietly. "What's it like?"

"What is what like?"

"Being normal."

"Well, my family didn't go around flinging knives at my back, my father doesn't sit around drinking blood, and until yesterday, I never had to shoot a military-grade demon with a magic wand because it was about to eat my talking cat."

"I'm a pwca," a voice called out from behind the counter.

"You better stay out of those coffee grounds," I growled.

Punkin jumped over the counter and then onto the table where Elain and I sat.

"Relax, I'm doing the inventory. How do you think the coffee cupboard got restocked?"

"I never thought about it," I said. "You've been doing it? What, you scoot up the stairs pulling a bag in your teeth?"

He tapped my ceramic coffee mug with a paw, and it disappeared.

"Hey! I still had half a cup."

"It's in the basement where the bags of bean are," he said. I could almost hear the snicker in his voice. "Pwcas are good at teleporting items short distances."

"When you go down to tap the bags to restock the cupboard," I said with a smile, "would you be so kind to teleport my coffee and cup back up here? Together. The coffee in the cup. Please?" The little snot would probably send them separately, and I'd have a mess to clean.

"Depends on how I feel when I get down there, and whether anyone calls me Fuzzbutt today."

"Your bum does look rather fuzzy," Elain said.

"See," I told him. "I'm not the only one who noticed."

"Hmfphf!" Punkin said and jumped off the table and headed into the cellar. He paused at the door and looked back our way.

"Did he just wiggle his bum at us?"

"Probably," I said. "All the witches in movies get owls and toads and chihuahuas for familiars. What did I get? A snarky cat."

My coffee mug popped back in front of me. There was coffee in it. And a layer of cat hair.

"Ugh! I will give him weight-control cat food for that." I went behind the counter and dumped the coffee into the sink.

"Want to take a walk?" Elain called. "Have a nose-about your new home town?"

"Sounds good. I've only been out once, and I didn't know how magical this valley was." I poured fresh coffee into a paper cup. "Need one?" Elain nodded, so I brought another out to pour her macchiato into.

Aunt Rose had the pixie sisters working on cleaning the tables.

"Do you need me to finish cleaning before we go?"

"Are you satisfied with how they cleaned your fancy coffee machine, dearie?"

I gave it an inspection and nodded.

"You've got your wand, too?"

I reached into my sleeve and pushed the magic in to make the wand pop out.

"Good girl. Go have fun and explore."

"Have a nice day, Lady Rhosyn," Elain said.

"Take good care of my girl," Aunt Rose said and waved us out.

"Any more demon hunts planned?"

"I should hope not," Aunt Rose said. "If you see any, Ebrel knows what to do."

"You think so?" I wasn't so sure.

"You'll be fine, dearie. Just blast it like you did yesterday until help arrives."

"Is that likely to happen again?"

"Let's hope not," Elain said and opened the door.

Two human tourists stood staring at the sign.

"I need a good cup of dark roast to function this early," the man grumbled.

"Sorry, guys," I said. He had a T-shirt on under his half-zipped jacket. I saw enough of the shirt to recognise the "Everything is bigger in Texas" slogan. "Wales gets up earlier than Texas. If you come an hour earlier tomorrow, I've ordered a big batch of aged Sumatra dark that should be in."

Elain had my elbow and led me away.

"You are talkative," she said. "I like that. Though not to extremes. Neirin talks too much and says little. The pixies talk..."

"Waaaaay too much," I said. We both shared a laugh.

"What does the name of your family's castle mean?"

"It's not a castle," Elain said with a chuckle.

"Looks like one."

"Well, it's a fortified manor house. More lovable than a drafty old castle and more reinforced than a modern estate. It started out as a wooden hill fort. Father says he had quite the time keeping the Normans out of it his first few centuries. After that, they knocked the old fort down. A century later, he rebuilt it, but as a more comfortable walled and fortified manor house."

"So what does Care Cindyfan mean?"

"Caer," she corrected, then laughed, "is the Welsh word for a hill fort, or a reinforced castle or manor house on a hill. Cigfran is Welsh for Raven."

"Caer Cigfran, Castle of the Raven. Sounds creepy enough to live in," I said. "Especially with parents like yours. Do you mind a personal question?"

We were out on the main road through town. The motorway ran two lanes wide, with cars ambling by on what I would have considered the wrong side of the road.

"Ask and I'll let you know," she said.

"What do you do?"

"Drink coffee and hang out with my new friend from America."

"Thanks," I said. "I'm glad you came down today. If you don't want to answer, that's fine. We've only known each other for less than a day."

"You deserve an answer," Elain said and steered us into an alley. Barti Ddu Pub was on one side. A sign with a guy who looked more like a pirate than a wizard swung above the doorway. The other side of the alley had a small grocer.

"Back here is a fae park," Elain said.

"Fae park?"

"No mundanes can reach it." She pulled me into a dead-end alley. Her own wand, with a dark ebony end and handle, slid out of her sleeve. She tapped the wall with it, and we were on the other side of the wall.

"Come on," she said. "The wall shifts back in a few seconds. We need to be in the park when it does."

Before me lay a lush garden. More trees, buzzing with pixies stood with their branches overhanging carved wooden benches. One resembling a dragon, with its wing raised, sat under a willow tree.

"That's my favourite," she said. "Io carved it."

"Really? It's beautiful. I'm afraid to sit."

"We won't break it." She slid onto the bench. "You asked about me. The entire village knows about Jasmine Dymestl's daughter returning home. I want to be your friend, so I'll share to keep us even. But this can never be mentioned to humans. And rarely in fae circles."

"That hush-hush?"

"Well, every fae knows my brother and I. They kind of know what we do."

"You said you're a team?" I remembered the knife throwing. "Of what? Secret agent spy assassin types?"

"Her Graces likes fae to know there is someone she can send if they really misbehave. However, no one mentions our profession in public." She gave me a shy smile. "You're not upset that I capture or kill people when needed?"

"Who employees you? Mercenaries?"

She shook her head. "The queens."

"Both of them... Fae and..."

"Exactly," she said. "When MI5 has issues with a human, one that needs more than just a grab or polish-off, we might get a call. When a fae goes renegade, we definitely get a call."

"You're not after me, are you?" A sudden pang of guilt spread in my belly. "I'm not sure I'm supposed to be a witch, or see ghosts. This is all so strange."

"So you think I've lured you here?"

"Did you?"

"No, silly girl." Elain laughed and held out her hand. I took it but watched her eyes.

"We don't kill friends," she said. "I want to be your friend. If Neirin and I were after you, you wouldn't know we were here."

"Why did you tell me what you do?" This seemed so weird... my newest friend was an assassin. "You work for MI...?"

"MI-13, the Ministry of Paranormal Activity and Citizenry."

"You've probably got all sorts of deadly stuff on you right now, haven't you?"

"You can see ghosts if they're here, right?"

"Hi, April!"

"Like my annoying ex-boyfriend in the tree? Yes."

"What are you two talking about?" Jake was sitting in the branches above us. A pixie darted through him as it flew fast past us. It didn't even notice Jake.

"Girl stuff," I said. "Where have you been?"

"Up at the castle," he said. "That guy with the knives has all sorts of cool toys. Knives, swords, and all black clothing. I think I saw at least a dozen knives on him. Cool, huh?"

I told Elain what he said. She bit her lower lip and then let her face go stone cold.

"Jake, you're not going in the ladies' rooms are you?"

"No, should I?"

"Remember what I said about watching me? The same goes for all women. Period. Got it?"

"You know I wouldn't..."

"Actually, that's why I liked you," I said. "You were one of the few men who didn't creep me out that way.

"Thanks... I think."

"Good. Now, do you mind if I have some girl time with Elain? Can you go find Sir Reginald and hang out with him?"

"He's with his mother at a cricket match in London. Some church or something... Lords Club."

"Go learn cricket, then," I told him with a wave. "Give me girl time, or I'll start popping you and your chickens."

"Okay! I'm going. Cricket it is." He winked out to wherever ghosts go.

I relayed that to Elain, who sat quietly and thought about the exchange.

"He was right above us? Any others about?"

I shook my head. "None that I can see. Jake and Sir Reginald said the fae queen issued a proclamation that the spirits were to leave me alone."

"You know," she said, looking around at the park, "you might be the only person who could sense if Neirin and I were coming after you."

13

Elain and I wandered through town. The pavement, the British term for what Americans called sidewalks, wasn't busy, though they weren't empty of tourists. I'd only been here three full days, and I was already considering myself a local.

"Ebrel Dymestl!" the shopkeepers called time and again. They'd come out and pull me into their stores. One woman took my hand and refused to let me go. The store was filled with skeins of yarn, hooks, long knitting needles. Almost every type of needlework or small sewing crafts were here.

"Your mum was such a sweetheart, Miss Dymestl," she said. "Me name is Haf. You probably don't remember. I was there on the first morning you worked the coffee." She leaned in and whispered. "I had one of the blue crystals for yer test. It plumb near vibrated off me bracelet, it did. I knew you were a strong one. And we heard about what you did with the demon in the ravine. Good show, dearie!"

There were more like her in almost every store. Shopkeeper

or clerk, they wanted to shake my hand and whisper which crystals they'd carried for my test.

"Is it always this bad when someone takes their test?" Elain and I were out in the street again and near the end of the main motorway.

"Not always," she said. "I only scored average on my crystals."

"Your skills lie in another area?" I asked.

Elain leaned in a gave me a side hug. I felt something hard under her sweater. Thin and flat. Much like the knife she had caught and thrown back at her brother.

"Definitely in other areas," she said and arched her eyebrows for a split second. "Oh, let's go in here. I see a new piece."

"Arthur's Artistic Emporium, sounds interesting."

"Ah, Lady Elain and Lady Ebrel, welcome to my gallery." The short man came out from behind the counter. Another gnome with a long pointed beard. His hair was long, but I caught glimpses of his ears. Not pointed like the ones on the Gnarly Recovery crew.

"Ah, still getting used to our town," he said, watching my eyes. "You'll see tonight when we can let our hair down, as you Americans like to say."

"Glamours," Elain whispered. "Humans are about."

"Ah..." I thought I understood.

"You have a new piece, Gneville," she said.

"You're not Arthur?"

"No, lass. However, every tourist loves a touch of ole King Arthur."

I laughed since I was one of those. "The stories are very British."

"French, actually," Elain said. "The Welsh have some old bardic tales from before the French ones, but they don't have all the romance and love triangles. Now, about that new painting."

"Ah, you have sharp eyes, Lady Elain." He walked towards the back of the store and gestured towards a painting. A large water-colour of the valley. The scene was bright, though it had a hard, gritty look to it and a soft flowing mix of the watercolours.

"My favourite artist strikes again," she said. "I love his blend of charcoal and watercolours."

"We're having postcards and prints made of this one," he said. "I fancy it one of his best works. We'll have an auction for the piece this fall once the tourist boom has subsided."

"I will be there," Elain said. "You may double my standing opening bid for this work."

Another work caught my eye. A carving similar to the dragon bench we had left back in the fae park. I stroked it with a finger. This was the same style of dragon carved in a light wood, standing on its hind legs, wings spread. The expression on the dragon said, "I'm awesome, and so are you."

"You like my work?"

I jumped.

"You startled me!" I slapped Io's shoulder. "Elain, have you —" I turned towards her and Gneville. The gnome was still explaining what he had planned for his newest watercolour. Elain's eyes lit up at Io, then darted down to his shoes. Her cheeks flushed and darkened.

"I guess you two know each other," I said.

"Of course," Io said. "Lady Elain keeps me in business painting more and more."

"Did you paint that?" I jerked a thumb at the watercolour and peered at the signature. Like any artist, it was difficult to decipher. With a closer look, I noticed the "I" and a squiggle that was probably the "oworth" in Io's full name. The large D in Dymestl was clear but the rest was again more of an artsy squiggle.

"You've seen my work before," he said. "In very rough form."

"When you walked me back from the top of the cliff and I fainted," I said. The bell on the door jingled, and the Texas couple walked in. I didn't add any more about pixies carrying me back or getting my wand.

"How is your car, Io?" Elain asked.

"A bit scratched," Io said. Gneville was off to assist the other guests. "Care for a bite and a pint?"

"Um… I don't have any money with me. I haven't had time to hit the bank in the village and get an account, nor convert cash to pounds."

"We'll run you by the bank after we eat," Elain said. "My treat for lunch."

"Aunt Rhosyn asked that I get you there today," Io said. "You're a member of the Dymestl family and have a trust account waiting on you."

"Huh?"

"Old money," Io said with a wink. "How do you believe my sister is able to hang out with that drifter boyfriend of hers in the desert?"

"So I don't have to rely on what my father sends me?"

"You won't be independently wealthy, but it's a decent sum," Io said. "I can live off of my share each year. I use my art to pay for my toys."

"Like your Mini? I'm sorry I slammed the ummm…" I glanced at Gneville and the Texans, who were talking big but spending little. "The beast… into it and ruined the paint."

"And dented the doors. And the roof." Io grinned. "Relax. Since it was an official hunt, though impromptu, Owain is requesting funds from MI-13 to cover the repairs. Aunt Rose said I'd best take it in and have the professionals do it, to make sure I didn't damage the Infernal with my tinkering."

"Let's head to Barti Ddu's before the tourists get hungry," Elain said.

Inside the pub was the typical dark, low-ceilinged pub atmosphere I'd seen in many British shows over the years. This pub had an old-time sailing theme. Mounted fish and nets hung from the ceiling. Oars and a large strip of canvas hung from the walls and ceiling. Thick rope was wrapped around the edges of the tables and the long wooden bar.

"Grab ye a seat anywhere!" a voice called out. "Oh, it's Lady Elain and Io. Bless me sails, it's Lady Ebrel. Do come in and take some munch and King Leer."

I glanced at Elain, puzzled.

"He means come in and have a pint and lunch."

"Aye," the bearded man said. He sported a well-trimmed black beard and wavy shoulder-length hair. He even wore a set of knee-length trousers and old-style buckled shoes. A colourful cord interlaced the open V of the shirt's neck, to about a quarter way down. The man looked almost too good to be a cosplayer, or a renfaire actor. Several gold chains around his neck and gold earrings in only one ear completed the pirate ensemble.

"Ignore the mayor and the Aussie there. They set a quiet spell on their table, so they don't want anyone to hear them."

"Mayor Yardley and..." Io paused, squinting into the dark. "Bryce Rustle, oh my. The mayor is very serious about getting a race in the valley."

"Isn't that the person... never mind," I said as we followed our pirate-themed host to a table near, though not next to, the mayor.

Barti passed around menus. "Rachel will be around in jiff to get your order. I warn you, me coffee is more tar and pitch than that sweet nectar you serve, girlie. I'd stick to a good pint here."

"Diolch."

Our round table had four chairs. Elain slid into the one farthest from the door and hung her purse from her knee, not on the back of the chair as I'd seen so many other women do.

Io took a seat next to her and didn't notice when her eyes slid to his face, then darted back to the menus.

I took the other seat next to Elain.

"Nice pirate theme," I said. "Barti plays the part well."

"He's not acting," Io said. "When the HMS Swallow had him cornered, a round of grape-shot took out some of his crew on the second broadside. He cast a glamour on the dead man and himself, switching places so it looked like he died. He retired from pirating, came back to the valley, and opened this pub. A century later, he hung his own name above the door."

"Wouldn't the authorities have something to say about a real pirate hanging out in Wales?"

"He paid his fines," Io said. "He hung around with your mum for a while."

I started to massage my temples again.

"Too soon," I said. "I'm still getting used to all this. I keep forgetting Mom is two centuries old."

"Three, actually," Io said.

I groaned at the reminder.

"Sorry about that. Habit," he added.

A pixie in an old-timey dress came to our table, order pad in hand. Her name tag said Rachel.

"Oh! Hi, Miss Ebrel!" she almost shrieked. Her hair was streaked with fiery orange highlights. "I want to try one of your new tornados. I'll be in tomorrow morning for sure. We're so glad you came back to the valley!"

I glanced down at the menu. The notoriety was starting to wear on me, at least from the pixies who could only think about the most commercial of the drinks I made.

"Are the fish and chips any good here?"

Io chortled. Elain touched my arm. "I've had the fish and chips in America. Once you try Barti's, you'll never want to return to the States for food again."

"I'll trust your judgement on the drinks as well," I said. "Order me something tasty to go with them."

Io got the fish and chips. Elain ordered a salad with chicken and tea.

"Now I feel like a pig," I said.

"I'll eat the other half of yours if you feel guilty about it," Io said.

A scraping of chairs interrupted us. The mayor stood, a scowl pulling his face down. He saw us watching and slid back into his political smile. The Aussie with him hesitated a beat before he took the mayor's outstretched hand.

"Oh, do try the fish, dear girl," the mayor said as he passed our table. "It's the best in the valley." He gave a long look at Rachel leaning through the order window into the kitchen before he nodded to us. He almost seemed to slither past our table on the way out.

"Hope his wife doesn't catch him looking at the pixies." Elain's eyes clicked methodically from the mayor to the gentleman left at his table.

"The pixies seem to be the eye candy of the valley," I said.

"It's rare they date out of their type," Elain said. "Most of them are aware of the effect they have on normal fae. Still, our mayor was never one to follow the rules."

"Mister Rustle?" Io stood. He offered his hand to the man. "I'm Io Dymestl."

"Ahh, I heard your name quite a bit, mate. MI-13 had quite a go with me last evening."

"You're welcome to join us." Io waved towards our table.

"Delighted, mate," Rustle said. "After the berating of MI-13, and the... attentions of that... mayor, I'd welcome pleasant company."

Io introduced Elain and I, using our formal Lady Elain and Lady Ebrel titles.

"Happy to meet you both," he said. "And thank you for being on site when that beastie I set Sir Reginald up with got loose."

"That was purely coincidental," I said. "I'd only received my wand a day."

"Inspector Jones had a glowing report of you," Rustle said. "I've helped wrangle those big boys into containers. Especially that one. I made sure to find a good one from the portal for Sir Reg."

"You know that was beyond a 4.6?" Io asked.

"Experimental grade, mate. They're allowed with the permits," Rustle said. "It's your Infernal cauldron he's in, isn't it?"

Io nodded. "We had to shave him down to make him fit."

"Again, thanks to both of you. The agents at MI-13 kept accusing me of boring holes in the cauldron. Had quite the time convincing them I didn't want a beast like that one running amok anywhere."

"They were concerned," Elain said. "Weren't you and Sir Reginald at odds several times on the race course?"

"On the pitch or on the track, we're competitors, dearie," he said and raised his glass of beer. "I've respected Reg since the first time I faced him on the cricket pitch. That man is a true legend. When he started driving the racers, I thought I was good enough to get some payback. He proved me wrong."

"Wrong enough to drill holes in the cauldron's protection spells?" Elain's voice had gone cold. Chill enough I didn't want to be on the other end of that statement.

"Look, miss," Rustle said, standing, "I had a day from... well, catching demons was more pleasant than what those MI POMs put me through yesterday. They accused me of doing in a man I truly respected. Afterwards, I had a slimeball politician kissing my backside to get my vote on the racing council to favour his idea. I don't need to take any more from a nice lady like yourself."

14

"My apologies, Mister Rustle," Elain said, softening her tone. "Sir Reginald was a dear friend of my family. It was our manor house he left the night he drove off the road."

"Oh, you're Macsen's little girl," Rustle said. "I sit with him on the fae-human racing council." He sat back down. "Forgiven if you'll let me buy you all a good Australian beer."

"I'm not sure it will go with my salad," Elain said. "Happy to accept, though."

Rustle ordered a round for us.

"I'll apologise on behalf of everyone else in the village," Io said. "We couldn't find anyone else to run for mayor. Mr Yardley won by default."

"If that's the least of your worries, you'll be fine, mate," Rustle said. "You should try living down the road from a demon portal. Driving like a bat out of Hades to contain the big beasties inspired me to go on the racing circuit. With a cauldron like yours, I fancy you're a racer too?"

"Only on the lower amateur circuit," Io said. "We've got

some smaller races here in the Welsh countryside, but only for fae drivers."

"That's what Yerdhead wants, an open race. A big spectacle," Rustle said. The pixie set pint glasses of beer in front of each of us. "We've got the votes to stop it in the Human-Fae Racing Commission meeting this week."

"Father is looking forward to that meeting," Elain said. "He's not fond of the idea. Neither is Lieutenant Colonel Reece."

"We're back to friends again?" Rustle asked. "Cheers, Big Ears!"

"Same to you, Big Nose!" Elain proclaimed. She raised her glass. Io and I followed along but looked at each other, sharing our confusion over the insults.

"Excellent," Rustle said. "You have been down to Oz, girl."

"Amongst other places."

"About the mayor's idea for a race," Io said. "You don't like the race idea?"

"Only dislike the mixing of mundanes and fae. And Yardley. Not fond of him, mate. He was trying too hard to leverage Reg's name into the event. He wants the race to put a feather in his own cap, not to honour a good man and a good competitor."

"So you want to block it? Aunt Rose said the valley wants tourism to grow."

"I've a seat on both the board of the Fae Racing Authority, and on the Human-Fae Racing Commission. We try to allow fae and mundanes to compete together only where there won't be a big spectacle if something goes wrong. Cricket is easy. As are hockey and football—the real kind, not your American pigskin variety."

"You mean 'go wrong' like an almost-military-grade demon escaping in a crash?" I shook my head at the idea of that happening where TV cameras would catch it.

"Exactly," Rustle said. "I keep trying to convince people to separate the few racing events we've merged into already. Break them to fae on one day, and mundanes on another. Like we do in Indy."

"Wait," I said. "I've been to Indy for the 500-mile race. There's only one."

"That humans see," Rustle said. "The fae race there on the night after the human race, once the main party is over."

"How do you keep the noise and the lights from being noticed?"

Rustle paused with his glass of beer almost to his mouth.

"She only got her wand two days ago," Io said.

"You're Jasmine's daughter?" He raised his glass again. "Magic skipped your mum, and it sounds like a double dose landed on you. If you're knocking demons apart in only two days, you'll be something else when you turn a hundred."

"Back to my question about magic to keep the Fae 500, or whatever it is called, hidden." I still wasn't comfortable with the idea of people around me living for centuries.

"MI-13 has their best illusionists around the track," Rustle said. "We keep the noise and lights inside. Set up a few rows of teleport portals inside the raceway, and the green shirts keep everyone from straying outside."

"Yellow shirts," I said. "The track security wear yellow shirts."

"The mundane ones, yes. Fae security wear neon-green shirts. Helps us know who belongs."

"So," Io said, "what are your thoughts on a Misty Valley Grand Prix?"

"Even if Yerd-bum weren't the one asking for it, I'd vote no," Rustle said. "I offered to put in a motion to add a semi-pro fae-only event here. But he only wants a mixed race, and a big one."

"We don't need mundanes around if a demon gets loose," Elain said.

"That's why we like closed tracks like Indy," Rustle added. "We keep our Brimstone patrols ready to take down any of them should one or two get loose."

"Sounds dangerous," I said. "Those cauldrons don't look sturdy enough to handle much of a wreck."

"They normally are. I saw the images of Reg's car," Rustle said. "There was tremendous damage, but no reason for the beastie to get loose."

"Except...?" Elain prodded.

"They showed me," Rustle said. "Accused me of trying to defeat a rival. Wouldn't believe me when I said it wouldn't be cricket to take him out that way. As a cricket player, I respect Sir Reg far more than to try a dangerous stunt like drilling the protection cauldron. I want to win the only good way—by having a better race than he does."

"Why are you here? Shouldn't the MI... what do you call them?" I glanced at Elain.

"Agents," she said.

"POMs," Rustle said. I cocked an eyebrow at him. "Australia started as a prison colony for Britain."

I gave a nod.

"Well, POM is a shortened form of 'Prisoner Of her Majesty.' The reason we have a large demon portal in Oz is that the fae council thought it would be a good place to send fae malcontents. That didn't work out. The fae prisoners rioted and opened the little demon portal wider. They thought they could get a demon or two that could help them."

"That didn't work?"

"The demons ate them," Elain said. "MI-13 had quite the time securing the portal. It only belches about once a week now."

"So you Aussies reversed the term POMs?" I asked.

"Exactly," Rustle said. "We're the free ones now. You Brits, especially those of you working for MI-13—" He held Elain's gaze for a few seconds. "—you're the prisoners."

He stood and drained his beer.

"When you get to the down under, mate, look me up." He held out a hand to Io. "I hope to see you on the course someday. You've got a heck of belcher in that cauldron of yours. If you've got the chops to race with the lads here, you'll be welcome down in Oz. Ladies." He tipped an imaginary hat to Elain and I.

Our pixie waitress, dressed in a cute pirate dress, brought our food out.

"Oh, mmm..." I said with the first bite of fish. "This is good."

"Just like your coffee," Elain said. "Fae cooks have a way with making their dishes special."

"Umm, I use a little jot of magic in my coffee." I started to blush.

"You don't believe Aunt Rose doesn't do the same with each tray of scones or pastries?" Io said. "I'm sure that Barti's mother does the same in this kitchen."

"What did you think of that exchange with Mr Rustle?" I asked after another bite and a drink of the dark English ale Io had ordered for me. "Oh, that goes well with this dish."

"I like Bryce," Io said.

"He's got an attitude," Elain added. "He knows I work with MI-13, so he might have been mardy about his early questioning. The agents in the Demon Division are an especially serious group. More so than most British government clerks."

"Would he have had reasons to bore into the cauldrons? I don't understand why someone would want one of those things to get out."

"Well, the mayor has been pushing for several years now on his race idea," Io said and glanced at Elain. "Have you heard of how recent that sabotage to the spells on Sir Reginald's car was?

I can see why the Demon Division might believe Bryce would. If he supplied the cauldron..."

"The ministry doesn't share info with me until I need to know it," she said. "If I get the call, I get everything I ask for. But only then."

"Why are you so interested in this?" Io reached across to take my second piece of fish. I slapped his fork away.

"Mine!"

"I believe she likes it," Elain said. "Never get between a fae girl and her fish and chips."

"Why do I want to know?" I shrugged. That was a good question. "Because Sir Reginald came to me. He's so nice. I just want to help him."

"You care," Elain said. "We all do. Reg was a friend to many of us, and role model to all of us."

"Was he poisoned?" Io asked.

"Owain hasn't shared the toxicology report with me," I said. Even the fries, or chips in Brit-speak, were yummier than I expected. "If he needs to interview Sir Reginald again, I must be there. I might find out. I'm surprised that MI-13 doesn't have some spell to speak with ghosts."

"They do. It's called a seance," Io said. "The ghosts are compelled to come and speak the truth. But the ministry doesn't like to use that unless they have a suspect. The ghosts say it's quite painful."

"Ghosts can feel pain?"

Io shrugged. "Ask your boyfriend."

"Ex-boyfriend," I said. "Dying put a big damper on our relationship."

A rather long chicken feather drifted down onto our table. Elain picked it out of what was left of my chips. They were yummy, but I was full enough I dare not eat more. She ran her fingers along it to straighten the plume, then tried to balance it point down on her finger.

"It's not a knife," Io said.

"We don't have spells on our weapons that can harm ghosts," she said. "Since this was ghostly, I wonder if it could be enchanted somehow."

"You going to tickle a renegade ghost to take them down?" Io and I both laughed.

Jake hovered by the buoy, poking at a fish hanging from the ceiling. His hand kept sliding through it.

"Anything can be a weapon," Elain said. "Do you mind if I keep this?"

"Why do you want a feather?"

"She can if she wants," Jake said. "Her brother is cool. And she's your friend. I've got plenty more."

"Jake says he's got plenty more, and you can keep that one."

Io looked at me strangely. "Your ex-boyfriend is a chicken?"

"No, his ghost is covered with feathers."

"Was he wearing a costume when he died?" Io's brows were scrunched together as he tried to comprehend.

"No." I smiled. "His accident was so ludicrous it would have been funny if he weren't dead because of it. He swerved to miss a mother opossum crossing the road right before an overpass. He was on his motorcycle. Idiot didn't have his helmet on."

"It wasn't against the law," Jake said defensively. He leaned in past me and ran his finger along the fries left on my plate, then licked his finger. "Wish I could feel or taste the real world."

"He swerved to miss the rodent, then hit a giant chicken?" Elain giggled. "I'm sorry. It's tragic."

"Not a giant chicken." I smiled to let her know it was okay. "He almost dumped his bike but managed to keep his balance. He hit the steel guard railing where it angled up from the ground, before it tied in to the concrete side of the overpass."

"Man, did I get some air!" Jake had his arms out, like he was riding his bike. I laughed and passed on what he said.

"Wheeee!" he said, reenacting his ride down the embankment.

"Do all ghosts remember their death?" Io asked.

"No. They seem to have a tough time remembering the day. It took Jake more than a year to remember anything beyond the opossum. Now he thinks it's funny."

"It was," Jake said and made motorcycle noises that only I could hear.

"He sailed into the highway below," I continued. "It wasn't very busy. The police said he might have survived if a truck hadn't been right there."

"Ouch!" Io said and winced. "Was the lorry driver injured?"

"Oh, he missed the cab of the truck," I said. "It was a farm truck, a regular semi-tractor trailer—"

"Reg says the Brits call it an articulated lorry," Jake said and threw his arms in front of his face. "CRASH! I went."

I laughed again and described Jake.

"The articulated lorry?" Elain and Io nodded, so I continued, "was hauling a flatbed trailer piled high with row after row of plastic cages of live chickens. Jake flew smack into them."

"Feathers and beaks and broken cages everywhere!" His ghostly form flipped and flailed around above us. More feathers fell, but only one turned real. Io plucked it out of his empty pint glass while I described Jake's antics above us.

"The crates slowed him down," Io said. "The chickens killed him?"

"No, the second truck behind the first one did. It smacked Jake, what was left of his motorcycle, and about four hundred chickens. He's covered in feathers and often has a chicken or two with him."

"I can have more," he said. "The truck smooshed a couple

hundred of them. I killed about eight hundred more when I slid in with my bike. I have an army of chickens at my command!"

"So you can open your own southern fried restaurant in ghost land?" I said and shared with Io and Elain.

"An army of chickens," Elain said. She had a twinkle in her eye. "I've never had to take out a giant rampaging chicken before. It's good you and Jake are here in case I need to."

"Tell her I'm at her peck and call!"

"Peck and call? I didn't know you could pun!" I said, laughing.

"British humour," Jake said. "Hanging out here with the British ghosts is rubbing off on me. Too bad we can't actually touch anything that we didn't die with." He held his hand out towards me. We both knew the gesture was futile.

"I'm sorry, Jake." I dabbed at my eye with my napkin. "I miss you too."

15

"The bank is down this alley," Io said.

"We're right in front of the bank," I said, my hand on the door handle, ready to pull.

"That's the mundane bank," Elain whispered. "Follow Io."

He walked us down a short alley. A dead end. He tapped the wall with his wand. I had another of those something-magical-just-happened sensations. The blank wall before us jumped behind us, and there was door in front, where only bricks had been before. The letters on the milky glass read: WBF.

"Ladies," he said, pulling it open and waving us in first.

Inside, a short hallway led to a lift. The doors swooshed open before we even reached them.

"Lady Elain, Lord Io, welcome," the short man said. He wore a shamrock-green suit and tie. Green patent-leather shoes completed the ensemble.

"Lady Ebrel," he said. "Welcome to WBF. We've been expecting you." The short fellow had a distinct Irish accent.

"Afternoon, Mike," Io said, stepping in behind me. The elevator interior was decorated with mahogany panels and brass ornaments. Mike tapped his emerald-green wand on the brass panel. It lit up the metal in glowing green "LL" letters. Lower level. Io had said the fae bank was under the human one. But what was WBF?

Iolo must have seen my puzzled look. "Welsh Bank of Fae," he said.

I tried to not stare at Mike, barely two feet tall, standing on platform meant for one his size. He wasn't quite at eye level with me. He had to be of another fae race I hadn't encountered yet.

There was little I could say that wouldn't mark me as a mundane girl just turned fae. Elain bit back a snicker as the elevator dropped.

"Go ahead, say it," she said. "Mike won't mind."

"Not at all, lass," he confirmed.

"Are there shamrocks on your socks?" I asked.

"Very good, miss," he said and lifted his trouser leg. Shamrocks and pots o' gold decorated his fine silk socks. "We leprechauns found our calling in taking care of other people's money. Me own father is head of investments at this branch. He'll be happy to help you keep your portfolio in line."

"Diolch," I said. I wasn't sure I could tell my father I was going to let a real leprechaun handle my investments.

"My pleasure, Lady Ebrel. I'll be in later for some of your coffee. Once you and Lady Rhosyn start the evening hours. The pixies have been raving about something called tornados."

"Ugh... Silly pixies," I said. "I'll never get an appreciation for a good espresso built in this village with them serenading the syrupy drinks."

"Trust me," Elain said, "you don't want pixies trying to be cultured. They are who they are. Syrupy drinks are their style."

The elevator doors opened before I could respond. The cavernous hall we had been deposited in was made of light marble streaked with gold accents. Individual teller stations that resembled offices more than counter stations lined the far wall. A single receptionist sat at a desk in front of us. Fiery red hair accented the shamrock-green blouse and jacket she wore. Pale-green eyeliner accented her green eyes.

"Welcome to the Welsh Bank of Fae," she said. The name plate in front of her read Siofra, WBF Investor Relations. "Lady Ebrel, we have been expecting you. I will find a banker to assist you."

That wouldn't be a problem, since only one office was occupied out of the half dozen before us. The leprechaun tapped her wand on a brass plate in front of her, angled so only she could read it.

"Mister Auric is available," she said.

A male leprechaun appeared on the platform next to Siofra's desk and extended his hand. "Right this way, Miss Ebrel. Would you prefer your friends to wait here?" he asked.

"No," I said. "I'm still learning what it means to be fae. Io and Elain are my advisors."

"Very well. My office is number four." He tapped his wand on Siofra's brass screen. "I will meet you in it." He waved us forward.

I glanced at Elain as we walked.

"Did that office grow? I distinctly remember only two chairs in each. Now there are three on this side of the table."

"You'll get used to the magic," Elain said.

"Now, Lady Ebrel," Auric said, sliding into the chair at the other side of the table, "we need to get your authorisation on several documents to open your trust account. Once we do, we'll get your wand updated with your account information."

"Oh, like how you paid at the pub," I said. Elain nodded. "I wondered why you pulled a debit card out of your sleeve."

"When mundanes are around, the wand appears as whatever mundane item you need."

"Here are the documents you need to read," Auric said and spun the brass tablet around. "When you're satisfied, please tap the 'accept' area with your wand."

"Oh, wow," I said after skimming the first page. "That is so much simpler to understand than what my father brings home for his accounts."

"We fae prefer to keep our records simple and concise," Auric said. "Eliminates the need for attorneys in all but the most strange of instances. If you agree, tap this box."

I pulled it out of my sleeve and tapped. The wand glowed, and I almost dropped it when a blip of purple light raced back and forth several times across the length of the wand.

"Excellent, we've programed your wand. You've got a full year's payout in your account now. Or would you like me to pull it back and release it month by month? That would give you a few quid more each month in interest."

"Yes, please," I said. "Though could I see the numbers before you do?"

"Of course." Auric touched the tablet with his own wand. "Touch the screen with your wand. Don't worry, only you will see the figures."

I whistled. "Between that and what my father gives me in my other trust, I don't have to work."

"Don't tell the pixies that," Io said. "They'll riot if they don't get their caramel tornados."

"I need to visit the café and experience one, myself," Auric mused.

"All of that syrup may not be for leprechauns," I said. "Do you prefer a good Irish whiskey?"

"Of course," Auric said. "I will trust your judgement when I stop by. You will continue with the café, will you not?"

"No worries," I said. "I learned long ago that I need to stay busy. Though some girl time, shopping, and lunching every week helps too."

"Definitely," Elain said. "We'll head to Cardiff next week if you like.

"If I may," Auric said. "Do you have a mobile with you?"

"Only the one I brought from the States."

"Tsk. That won't do at all. You'll miss out on alerts and news on the fae network."

"You need to switch," Io said, nodding. Elain agreed.

"I assume it won't drain my month's funds?"

"A modest fee," Auric said. "We'll credit you back for your old phone and recondition it for a mundane. I can even pull your information and files from it. Tap the accept on the screen..."

My wand was getting a workout. I scanned the agreement, again a simple one, and hit accept.

"I will return shortly with your new phone. This is the popular model, and we can match it. A few moments, please."

He stepped back and faded from view.

"Does everyone except me know how to teleport or whatever?"

"The leprechauns do it as part of their innate magic," Elain said. "Most buildings have wards that make teleports stop at the door outside. With mundane tourists around, everyone is careful about when and where they teleport to."

"It's difficult," Io added. "Most fae can only teleport a few feet away. Except the leprechauns. It's a unique talent to them. That's why the leprechauns license their teleport crystals to major events."

"Like what that Bryce Rustle said they did at the Indianapolis 500?" That made sense. "Does every race in the fae world have a specialty?"

"Yes. Pwcas are excellent at a host of little things," Elain said. "That's why they are hired for in-home and on-site tasks. A lot of construction and cleaning. Pixies, though flighty, have excellent memories, balance, and dexterity. Their magic allows them to shift from human to pixie. In human form, they make good counter and service employees."

"And messengers," Io added. "At least until the interfaeweb grew out of the internet. Now, pixies are service oriented."

"I DON'T CARE!" a familiar voice shouted.

"Mister Mayor, please," another Irish accent piped up. "We have done what we can to secure your funding. Please step back into my office so we can discuss this matter."

"We've discussed enough already!" Yerdleh Yardley said. "I pushed the town council to hire your bank to handle funding for the Dewsberry Misty Valley Race, and we only have a tiny balance of twenty quid?"

"As I explained, Mister Mayor," the leprechaun said, exasperation evident in his tone, "you need to get final approval from the human and fae racing councils before we can secure larger donations."

"And I need several major backers before I can convince the racing council to consider us for a combined race."

"Please, let us step back into my office so we don't disturb our other clients," the leprechaun urged.

"No, I believe we're through today. I will speak to the council about terminating your contract."

"As you will, Mister Mayor."

Auric came back and slid a phone just like my old one across the table.

"Give it go, miss. It should have a full charge."

I tapped it on, entered my passcode. "Looks just like my old one."

"Look in the upper left by the clock," Auric said. "See the shamrock? Tap that for the interfaeweb."

I did, and my phone chimed. In triplicate. Io and Elain each reached for their own. A message appeared. I had an invitation from R,LE.

"That's Rhian, Lady Edernyion," Elain said. "Mother had Jonathan sent invitations out. She wanted to do something for Sir Reginald. A remembrance service."

"Like a wake?" I asked.

"Similar," Elain said. "Some sombre moments, then lots of drinking in his memory."

"Tomorrow evening," Io said. "I can drive you up."

"You'll be there too, I take it?" I asked Elain.

"Of course," she said. "Do you have much formal wear?"

"Is it black tie?"

"No, though you'll want more than yoga pants and a long sweater," she said. "We can spend the afternoon shopping. There are some boutiques in the village with some nice dresses."

"And shoes," I said. "A new dress needs better shoes than my flats."

"I'll go check on my Mini," Io said. "I enjoy your company, ladies, but even I'm not crazy enough to go clothes shopping with two women."

"Smart man," Auric said. I agreed, smiling knowingly at Elain.

Three hours later, we were back at Mystic Brews. Even though tea time was in full swing, there was an open table. Elain grabbed it while I ran my purchases up to my room. Punkin was curled into a fuzzy ball on my bed. He cracked one eye open, then slammed it shut.

"Shh! Cat is sleeping," he said.

"Get your lazy bum up," I said.

"Why? The joy of being stuck in cat form is that everyone expects me to sleep."

"Well, don't get fur on my new dress," I said. "At least not until the wake for Sir Reginald tomorrow."

"We're going to Castle Raven again? Excellent!"

I put my hands on my hips. "Why should I take you? Did you get an invitation?"

"Check yours," Punkin said. "I don't have access to the inter-faewebs until I serve out my century."

I looked closer at the invitation. Towards the bottom, a small line read, "Well-behaved and courteous familiars welcome."

"Looks like you're out of luck," I said. "Only well-behaved and courteous familiars are invited."

"Hah! I'll be on my best behaviour," he said.

"That may not be near enough," I said. "Lady Rhian will use you for her after-wine snack if you hack a hairball on her dress."

"It was coffee grounds," Punkin said. He stood, stretched, then turned several times and lay back down. "And her proper address is Rhian, Lady Edeirnion. Earless is not a real title, so it becomes Lady instead. If Edeirnion were a duchy, she'd be Rhian, Duchess Edeirnion. When someone has a full title, you never put lord or lady in front of their first name. For the wife of an earl, you use Lady and the name of the commote they manage. Call her either Rhian or Lady Edeirnion. Good thing I'm going with you. You'll offend half the guest list before the night is over."

"So, why am I Lady Ebrel, then?"

"You are a member of the fae royal line," Punkin said. "Therefore you have an honorific of 'lady' before your first name. Her Grace, the Queen of the Fae, has not granted you a real title, such as Duchess Lattes. When she finally does, you'd then be like Rhian. Your correct address would be Ebrel, Lady of Lattes."

I giggled at the thought of getting a title because of how I made espresso.

Once I made it back downstairs, Elain already had tea service waiting for me.

"Ebrel!" Nia called. "Can I try to make a tornado?"

"Tomorrow morning," I said.

"But Mister Tex wants one now."

"Greetings, miss," the Texan said from a nearby seat. "Bryce here has been telling me about your coffee. I hoped I could convince you."

"My apologies," Bryce said, standing and offering his hand again. "This is Lady Ebrel of the Dymestl family. Ebrel, this is John Calhoun and his wife, Sarah. John is on the other half of the racing board I'm on."

"I hear there's magic in your macchiatos," Calhoun said and gave me a wink. "I'd like to see what that tastes like."

"Then I better be the one to make it for you," I said. "Nia is still training. Or can I interest you in the best espresso you'll find this side of Italy?"

"A tornado," Calhoun said, then he lowered his voice. "Else that young lady won't stop pestering me about them."

"Excellent," Bryce said and turned to me. "Will you be at the wake tomorrow? I've gotten permission to bring John and Sarah to the caer to meet everyone. We've got the human side of the HF council in for the race meeting, and John is president of the commission."

Mundanes at Castle Raven?

"Father said he's looking forward to the commission meeting," Elain said.

"He and Rhodri are both concerned about the mixing of the race," Calhoun said. "I want to learn more about Sir Reginald's accident before I make my recommendation. I look forward to meeting your um... Misty Valley folks."

Elain exchanged a glance of worry with me. Even though I'd only known fae existed for a few days, there were several mundanes going to Raven Castle to meet us all? That would be interesting.

❧ 16 ❧

Io's new demon behaved better, or so he said. Still, I white-knuckled on the armrests all the way up the mountain. Sudden surges in acceleration happened all too often. Notably when we were on curves.

"Is he trying to kill us?" I asked, unable to keep the tension out of my voice.

"No, just escape," Io said. "There is a three-month breaking-in period when we get a new demon installed."

"He seems aggressive," I added as Io manhandled the car around the first of three hairpin turns in a row.

"Not as bad as women shopping," Io said with a chuckle. "How did you fare on your excursion?"

"Pretty good," I said. "Well, there is always that one shopper."

"Hmmm... clothes shopping in Misty Valley, and based on your tone, you must be referring to Gemma de Yardley." He shifted his tone into one Americans would call hoity-toity and spoke with a strong nasal quality. "Oh, miss, I say... I say I haven't got all century to select these shoes. I must have something to go with my designer handbag that matches my designer earrings that I spent not a small amount of my husband's trust fund on. Do please pry yourself away from the riff-raff and cater to my needs."

"That was her!" I had to let go of the armrests and wrap my arms around my belly, I was laughing so hard.

"She's one of Misty Valley's characters," Io said. "Count your blessings she hasn't been in for coffee."

Elain had invited us to arrive early, that way I could change in her apartment. The way I was fighting adrenaline as Io attempted to keep his new demon under control, I might need another shower.

"Remind me to ride with Aunt Rose for the trip down."

"You don't like my driving?"

"I'm not too wild about your engine," I said. "If you get him calmed down, we'll see about another ride."

"Once I get a proper chance to get him on some open road, I'll work the kinks out of him."

Elain met us inside when Jonathan answered the door.

She was already wearing her dress for the evening. Off the shoulder, with a smart jacket that gave her sleeves. She had cautioned me against anything sleeveless. "Someplace to keep your wand," she said. "The men have it so much better with jackets and pockets."

Io had his jacket folded over his arm, and his tie was loose but tied. He'd only need a few seconds to go formal. I needed a good half hour.

Neirin was waiting at the top of the stairs and headed down as soon as the door shut. I sucked in a breath when I saw him. The thin moustache was still above his lip. The long wavy hair fell to his shoulders. He wore a jacket with an Italian flair of old. He looked like he should have a long thin sword in hand to say—

"You killed my father..." he said, dropping into a sword stance, arm out towards me without the blade.

"He does that all the time," Elain said, rolling her eyes. "Don't get him started. He's seen the movie at least a hundred times."

"Lady Ebrel," Neirin said, taking my hand and laying a kiss on it. "The honour is truly mine."

"I... uh..."

"Another woman left speechless at my mere presence," he said, lifting his chin. "Come, Lord Io, let us retire to the weapons hall so that the ladies can prepare for the party without gawking at our manliness."

"Excuse us, please," Io said. His eyes lingered on Elain for a moment. "I, um..."

"Just go," Elain said. "Get my brother out of here before he makes us keel over with laughter at his antics. I don't want to take the time to get this dress pressed again."

Once we made it to the top floor, Elain tapped her wand to unlock her door. I expected a larger version of the single room I had at Aunt Rose's. Instead, a full apartment spread out before me. The main area was an open-concept living, kitchen, and dining area. Glittering stainless steel appliances graced the kitchen. She even had a little home-brew espresso machine on the counter.

"Oh, wow! So much bigger than the tiny room Aunt Rose gave me. And antiques are not lining every foot of open space."

"Rhosyn is a bit of a pack rat," Elain admitted.

White furniture brightened the living area. Her walls weren't the sombre wood of the rest of the manor house. Small and large pieces of art brightened the off-white plaster. Much of the art was of a familiar watercolour and charcoal mix.

"Wow! You like Io's art. Or is it Io you like?"

Her eyes dropped, and she tried to hide a smile.

I smiled too. "If I were in the human world, I'd ask if you thought dating someone four or five time your age was excessive."

"We fae live much longer than mundanes," she said. "And we're not dating."

"Not yet. Want me to prod him to ask?"

"No! I mean..."

"He has to figure it out on his own. I know."

"You can change in my bedroom," she said to change the subject. "There are mirrors in there."

"Do vamps not like mirrors?"

Elain shrugged. "My parents never have issues with them. It's probably a folk tale to help hide the nature of the local vamps..." Her voice dropped a few octaves to mimic a classic vampire movie. "If you can see us, we're not vampires."

"You said earlier, or was it your mother, that they adopted you after the blast in Swansea? What was that?"

"A right bloody awful mess. Bernard and Betrys Dewsberry had an awful fight that night. No one knows who drew their wand first. The conflagration was epic."

"Did Sir Reginald's father have temper issues?" I slid my little black dress on. I had opted for something that could double both as casual outing or date wear, and a more sombre event like tonight. Fortunately, the weather was chill enough I could substitute black tights for my yoga pants. I wasn't sure if the castle would be draughty and chill. I wasn't trying to use my little black dress to find a date, so tights would work instead of hose.

"Bernard? Not at all," Elain said and closed the zipper on the back of the dress for me. "Betrys, however, was known for her temper. Mother says that woman would be quiet, with a fierce glare in her eye. Then she'd unleash a tirade that could knock the moon out of the sky."

"Hmm... sounds like the qualities of Reg's mother," I said and slid my new shoes on. Closed toe with heels that weren't too high or too thin. I'd been around enough to desire comfort instead of trendy style. "I love how opposites attract like the Dewsberrys. Did they have magical specialties? I mean, everyone seems to have a specialty."

"I forget what Betrys's specialty was, if I ever knew," Elain said. Her own dress was longer than mine, with slits on one side. She, too, wore tights and practical yet dressy shoes. "Bernard, however, is one of the heroes of the Queen's Company. He and the lieutenant colonel had quite the run of exploits. MI-13 trained us with techniques and lessons from some of their capers."

"The Queen's Company?"

"The predecessor to MI-13," Elain said. She pulled her wand out of her sleeve enough to check its availability, then slid it back in again.

"Do you always check your wand like that?"

"Ever seen a gent pat his pockets when he goes to leave?"

"Wallet and keys and phone," I said. "Yeah, almost every guy I've seen does that."

"I like to make sure I'm prepared."

"Umm..." Her dress wasn't skintight, however, it wasn't loose nor baggy either, and the smart jacket she wore to complement it was also form fitting. "Do you even have room for a knife in that get-up?"

"Well, I do use magic to help." She grinned. "However, let's just say that I carry more than I hope to ever need."

"Neirin too?" I chuckled. "Don't answer. I don't want to know what he carries with him."

Elain used her wand to lock the door to her apartment.

"Get your wand out, Ebrel."

"What for?"

"I'll add yours to my lock. That way if the party gets to be too much, you can retreat to a quiet place to hang out." Her wand glowed again with a spark of dark purple, almost black light. "Tap here."

I did as she requested. My wand glowed for a second. Elain tapped the door again.

"Try to open the door."

The handle turned easily, and the door swung open.

"You don't have to touch the handle, just the door," she added.

"There you are," Punkin said. He walked down the hall toward us. "I was about to starve out here."

"How did you get here?" I asked accusingly.

"Hitched a ride with Rhosyn," he said. "Some witch you are, leaving your familiar behind." Aunt Rose rounded the corner and headed our way.

"I needed girl time," I told Punkin. "And you're not a girl."

"I'm cute, fuzzy, and fun to be around. Every girl should want a familiar like me."

"Am I really stuck with him for a century?"

"Sorry, but yes," Aunt Rose said. "My sister placed a geas on him, and it has spread to you."

I squinted at her. "Did you come to find me? Or just to deliver Fuzzbutt?"

"Both, actually." She started patting her sleeves. "Wherever did I put my spectacles? I hope I didn't leave them at the café."

I tapped the top of my head and pointed to hers.

"Oh, thank you, dearie. So nice to have you around. The pixies always laugh at me when I go looking for stuff." She slid her spectacles on and glanced around. "Oh, where did he get to? Sir Reginald was to come with me."

"You came to find me?" I reminded her gently.

"Oh, yes. Rhian, Lady Edeirnion, asked if you could stay near

Sir Reginald for at least the first half of the evening. People will want to give their condolences, and they'll seek you out in hopes you can see him."

"So I'm supposed to translate for him?" I shrugged. "At least I'll be useful."

"And my brother might leave you be," Elain added. "You're the new girl, so he'll play the smitten fool tonight. Unless you're in an official capacity."

"Thanks for the warning." Just what I needed, a vampire assassin playing the love-struck fool over me while I acted as interpreter for a gentlemanly British ghost at his own wake. My new surreal life.

The sombre part of the wake itself wasn't long. Macsen, Lord of Edeirnion stood on the stage at one end of the grand ball-room. A few hundred fae of various stripes were there. Many sported what I learned were cricket caps. Almost like American baseball caps, though with a shorter brim and a tighter fit, more like a skull cap.

"The Aussies prefer a looser version," Sir Reginald told me. He gestured to where Bryce Rustle stood with several others sporting the wool caps along with their jackets and dress slacks. "The English, Scottish, and Irish all prefer the tighter fit."

From the stage, Macsen gave his recollection of several times when Sir Reginald had exemplified the character traits that got him both knighted and earned his many Spirit of Cricket awards.

"I had to bow out of the Spirit award," Sir Reginald said to me. "The community was most gracious, though they were quite resolved, and I had to be rather forceful that I would accept it no longer. Other players deserved it far more than I."

A gentleman with a thick bushy moustache and long side-burns that ran down his cheeks, stretching almost to his mouth, stood next. Mutton chops.

"Forgive me, my friends," the man said. "I have been..." He

cleared his throat. His suit and tie had an odd cut to them. More like an old-style military uniform.

"I promised my dear friend, Bernard Dewsberry, that I would be his friend through thick and thin. So when he and his wife had their little tiff, there was naught I could do but bring young Reginald into my care."

"Ah, the lieutenant colonel," I whispered. He would look better in one of those old British Army helmets from a century before, I decided. Then I realised his facial hair and clothing suggested that. I had seen the style in several movies and shows.

"Rhodri is an excellent role model," Sir Reginald remarked. "A sterling example of a British gentleman and a member of the Queen's Company. He and father were partners, much like your friend Elain and her brother are in MI-13. I owe much of who I am to Rhodri."

"As many of you know," the colonel continued, "I have spent the past months travelling the world to search for my good friend and foster son. I dreaded the worst, and that has come to pass, unlike my fears that he had been kidnapped and taken off to sea... Did I ever tell you about the time Bernard and I travelled with Davy Jones to..."

"Rhodri," Macsen said, setting a hand on the man's shoulder. The lieutenant colonel pulled himself straight and set his shoulders.

"Right, enough time to tell stories later. I invite you all to raise a glass to the best of men, to the best of cricket. To my foster son, Reginald!"

Everyone in the ballroom was already standing. Several cries of "Huzzah!" and "Pip, Pip!" sounded. The colonel raised his own drink. The crowd hoisted their glasses.

"To Sir Reginald!"

"Please, my friends," Macsen said. "Make use of the various bars around the room. Pick your poison, as the Americans say.

I've been told that Sir Reginald's spirit is among us with a translator. However, please don't crowd Lady Ebrel if you wish to pay your respects to him."

The lieutenant colonel had his eyes on me and approached.

"I'm too misty eyed to say much, lass," he said. "If you and Reg could stand by his cricket gear, I will stay on the other side of the room. Everyone here will want to stop and talk. Best that we be on opposite sides and keep the crowds dispersed."

"Always the military strategist," Reg said warmly. "Please give the old fellow my kindest regards."

"Reginald is grateful, Lieutenant Colonel."

"I'm sorry, say that again, my dear." He cocked his head to the side. "I have lost the hearing in my right eye."

"You mean ear?" I tried to project my voice.

"What? Oh, yes. My right ear. Never been the same since Bernard and I chased those sea hags down. Nothing like a cauldron explosion to set one's sight and hearing all askitter."

I repeated my earlier comment from Sir Reginald.

"Please, my dear, call me Rhodri." He fished in his breast pocket, and I felt a surge of magic. "Oops!" He pulled the ugly end of a long metal tube, flared open, from his inner breast pocket, then slammed it back down. "No worries. I'll find it." After a few more tries, with more magical surges into his pocket, he pulled forth a handkerchief to dab his eyes. He turned away, straightened his shoulders.

"It will be a difficult night, but one we must endure. Carry on, Lady Ebrel. I have the utmost confidence in you."

"He is shaken, poor chap," Reg said. Even in ghost form, his eyes were misty. "If he's pulled his elephant musket out, he's not feeling his best. He's never been that careless with his firearms."

"He's got a musket in that pocket? How?"

"Just like where we place our wands," the ghost said. "Well, I don't have a wand any longer. Don't seem to need one in this realm."

"Okay, then," I said, making a mental note to do just what the colonel said and stay on the opposite side of the room from him.

17

Owain wandered up next. He held a hand out with a dark crystal on it. I sensed another surge of magic.

"A silent spell is around us," he said. "Is Sir Reginald here?"

I nodded and tilted my head towards where his spirit floated.

"Feels so odd looking off into nothing," Owain said and shifted his eyes to me. "Sir Reginald, the toxicology tests came back." The inspector's eyes flipped back to the empty space next to me. "That isn't much better. Speaking to Sir Reginald and looking at a young woman." He closed his eyes. "Please tell him that the tox tests were negative. They found no poisons or unexpected substances in any of his tissue."

"Please, my dear," Reginald said, "ask him if there was any sign of magical influence. I was not my normal self that night. Something was causing me to doze off at the wheel."

"Nothing we could find," Owain said after I relayed the request. "But then, having an almost-military-grade demon leak brimstone and demonic ichor on him for a year will have clouded or washed any evidence of spell tampering. We are lucky that the tox isn't affected by it. Nasty stuff, demon ichor."

After that conversation, I endured about an hour of various people stopping to chat with Sir Reginald. When one would approach, the others waiting would give plenty of room around us. Almost as if they didn't want to step on Sir Reginald's spirit.

Since I was standing in front of the main display of his cricket gear, many of the wake-goers would look at one of the large photographs of Sir Reginald in his cricket gear instead of me.

Several of the leather-wrapped cricket balls rested on the table, and several of the flat-sided cricket bats were laid on an old canvas equipment bag. "RD" was scrawled onto the bag in ink. The letters were faded, but they'd been written in a bold hand. His shoes, white trousers, and white shirt with the logo were all laid out with a flair for detail. The uniformed matched what I saw him wear in his spectral form.

"Is that what you wore when you crashed?" I asked during one interlude between visits.

"Not at all. I dressed much as the men you see here tonight," he said. "I suspect we wear in death what we're most known for." He pointed towards where Jake floated near the lieutenant colonel, with his leather biker jacket, still covered in chicken feathers as he leaned in to listen as Rhodri extolled another of his adventures.

"Your man, there, Jacob, is known most for his demise. So he wears that in the afterlife."

"Makes sense," I said and recalled to the other spirits I had encountered. "You're the first famous ghost I've met. Everyone else was pretty normal."

During another gap in those seeking to say a few words to Sir Reginald, I scanned the crowd. Yerdleh Yardley, Mayor of Misty Valley, had that Texan, Calhoun, and two other men cornered by one of the racing memorabilia tables. Trophies and photos of Reg near his various racers lined the display.

"What are those two chatting about?" I muttered.

"The mayor is trying to convince the human commission members to support his new race," Jake said. "I eavesdropped when I did my last circuit of the room."

"Ah," Sir Reginald said. "I hope Macsen and Bryce can talk sense to them. Mundanes are keen to get exposure to magic. If Bryce can't keep that Texan against the idea, I'm afraid the lieutenant colonel may be inclined to wave his elephant musket around to make the point."

Yardley was gesturing with his champagne flute and sloshed most of it out of his glass. Once he realised what he'd done, he set it on the display table next to a large photo of Reg with a green-and-red sports car. He pulled his wand from a sleeve. With a wave of it towards one waiter, two more flutes of bubbly rose from the tray and drifted towards the mayor.

He took both from the air and offered one to the Texan. Calhoun narrowed his eyes and shook his head. Without a word, he turned away from the mayor and drifted into the crowd. Yardley kept speaking with the two humans.

"How are you holding up?" Elain asked. "Didn't mean to interrupt."

"No worries," I said. Sir Reginald flashed a smile and drifted away towards his foster father.

"Does the mayor like to show off?" I asked.

"Was he doing his 'levitate the drink' bit again? He always does that to impress new folks. He's one of the best at telekinesis, moving objects. I've seen him juggle half a dozen balls with only his wand."

"What have you been doing?"

"Well," she said, a grin growing on her face, "remember that annoying woman from the boutique where we found your dress?"

"Mrs Yardley?"

"Oh, Io gave you his impression of Gemma de Yardley, did he?" Elain laughed. "He nails her to a T. She was doing her best to flirt with my brother. I had to rescue him. She's chasing Rustle now."

"Why is she de Yardley? The de isn't part of Yerdleh's name is it?"

"She used to be de Umple before they married. She drops her maiden name as often as possible to remind people of her station. Our family is the only one of higher rank in British nobility in the valley."

"What chance does a poor little American like me have against titles like those?" I must have rolled my eyes based on the way she giggled.

"Don't underestimate your titles, Ebrel," Elain said. "You're of the Dymestl family. The queen of the fae is a Dymestl. On the fae side, you outrank everyone in the valley except Rhosyn and Io."

She glanced around to make sure no one was close.

"I noticed Owain was first in and had a silent gem active," Elain said, barely above a whisper. "News?"

"Well, he didn't say I couldn't share." I could put two and two together to know the silent gem was to keep others from hearing the details. I steered us through the displays of Reg's awards, trophies and plaques from both his cricketing—if that was even a word—and his time racing.

"He does have a lot of awards."

"Quite a few, yes," Elain agreed. We found a secluded corner, next to the stage where Macsen had stood. "Now spill it."

"Tox report came back negative," I said. "Reg asked if there was any magic residue. Said he felt too groggy for no poison."

"Let me guess," Elain said. "The demon iched all over the car and body, so no magic found."

"Happened before?"

"Yes," she said. "Doesn't take much of a demon to leave a pool of demonic ichor. If he had a four-plus demon in that car, and it was leaking for a year..." She shook her head.

"Someone wanted him dead and wanted to cover their tracks."

"Ladies," a familiar Aussie accent called out.

"Speak of the devil," I breathed.

Elain shot me a look. It showed she was thinking what I was thinking. A competitor, and one with ready access to a demon.

"You must forgive my tardiness," Bryce said. "That inspector fellow has been monopolising my time. He seems to believe I wanted my good friend to race in the afterlife."

"Yes, you and Yerdleh seem to be at the top of the suspect list," Elain said.

"Don't you go starting too, lass." He took a long drink from his beer and stared at her across the glass. "I've had quite the time explaining, first to your mates down in MI-13, and tonight to that Owain chappie, that I admired Reg. Racing isn't about grudges. It's a test of skill. Against your own car, against the course, and against the other racers."

"The track can get heated," I said. "Trading paint and such."

"That's American racing," he said. "Those good old boys like to bump a lot. That's not saying we won't, but a racer like Reg doesn't have to bump. He always raced clean and rarely finished less than top five. He was talented behind the wheel."

"Do you think someone who couldn't beat him on the track would take him out some other way?"

"Perhaps, but most of my racing mates would want to do it on the race course, not on a deserted mountain road."

"And you brought him the souped-up super demon," I said. "No wonder the authorities want to ask you questions."

"Your MI-13 men inspected the cauldron at our facility, and

again at customs on both sides of the world," Bryce said. "It passed every time. I can't say when the protective wards got zapped, but I've got the paperwork and inspection reports to show she was fine when she left Oz."

"What about Yardley?" It was a thought I just had. "Would he have wanted to bump off Sir Reginald?"

"Bump on the track, definitely," Bryce said. "Ever since he got benched for his attitude towards the Dewsberry spinner, he has been looking for a way to get even with Reg. Even tried to climb up the racing circuit and take him on."

"What happened?"

"It wasn't pretty," Bryce said with a smile. "He needed to come up through the bottom leagues. They get aggressive down there."

"Someone teach him a lesson?"

"Oh, yes," Bryce said with a chuckle. "Some of my mates in Oz didn't take kindly to his style of driving. What's worse, one of the pre-race auto inspectors found a wand stashed in the steering column. Yerdhead claimed it 'fell in there' during maintenance. Fat lot of good that did him."

"He used it during the race? Isn't that against the rules?"

"Most definitely against the rules. He had won his last race in Perth's circuit, but one of the other drivers said it felt like he was pushed several times when Yardley was tailing him. There are some dead areas in the magic-detection zone out there, but we don't tell anyone. Our drivers all respect the rules and self-police if one of them gets aggressive."

"What happened after they found the wand?" I asked.

Elain stifled a chuckle.

"I pulled his racing card and handed him a lifetime ban," Bryce said. "Banned from one country, you'll never race in any other. So he slunk back here and ran for mayor."

"We even tried to get Bob the Troll to run against him."

Elain sighed. "No one wanted the job, so he won the election. With only one vote."

"His own?" I looked at Gemma de Yardley, still trying to get Bryce Rustle's attention. "Not even his wife?"

"No one else voted in that race. Only one vote was cast in the mayor's race."

"After we disqualified him from racing," Bryce said, "that's about the only win he's had. Ah... If you will excuse me, ladies. I see a man I need to talk to about another demon."

"Not another military-grade one?" Elain asked.

"Learned my lesson with Reg," Bryce said. "This one is only a 4.3. Anything bigger than that is going to the military. If they don't want it, then we'll see if a pro-race team does. G'day."

My smart watch buzzed. I glanced at it. Io texted. Lesson time: Where is your familiar?

"How do I find Punkin?" I asked. Count on my trainer to interrupt girl time with a magic lesson.

"He's your familiar," Elain said. "Close your eyes and think of him. Like you think of your wand when you retrieve it."

"Oh, fiddle beans! He's in your kitchens rummaging for stuff. He better not be wasted on coffee grounds again. How did he get in there?"

"I forgot to exclude him when I set the lock to let you in," Elain said. "My fault for not remembering you have a familiar."

"That little stinker!"

"I'll go tweak him," Elain said. "You stay here with Reg."

No sooner had she left than Yerdleh Yardley stepped in front of me.

"Is Sir Reginald here?"

"He is about, but not with me," I said. Even though I dreaded the conversation, I knew it had to happen. "He said he'd watch for me by the cricket table and return if I were there."

"I should like to leave my regards with him, if I might, young lady." The mayor had an almost-empty glass again. I cursed my luck for not having one at all as we made our way back to my former station.

"Let me get you a drink, my dear. You must be parched after all this conversation." With a wave of his wand, two glass flutes started drifting through the crowd. One lady I had not met backed into the glasses.

"Whoops!" the mayor said. His wand flicked like an orchestra conductor's, and the glasses spun and wove a staggered path. They dived and scooped the champagne out of the air. "There. Got it all. Not a wasted drop."

"You have some talent," I said. No reason to not give him praise for it. I'd noticed that, while working my old coffee jobs, most people just wanted someone to notice them. Doing so wouldn't hurt too much. Elain would come back and scare him off. The glasses drifted close, and the mayor handed one to me.

"Oh dear," Sir Reginald said, appearing behind the mayor. "I suppose we have to let him know I've returned. Better get on with it."

After a few rounds of the same old platitudes, the mayor moved to his primary goal.

"Would you, dear chap, consent to lending your name to the Misty Valley race we're working on?"

Sir Reginald's lips moved sideways in a weird expression as he considered. I could see the conflict in him.

"I want to help the valley," he told me. "But what Yerdleh plans won't do that. Not with demons in the cars."

"He's concerned about the ambitious nature of an open fae and mundane race," I said while Sir Reginald was still searching for a way to be polite about the subject.

"Diolch, Lady Ebrel. Sometimes direct is best," Sir Reginald said, watching the mayor's reaction.

"Sounds like he's been talking to the Aussie chap," Mayor

Yardley lamented. "I can assure Sir Reginald that nothing of the sort will happen. We'd limit the cars to 3.5-level demons and have MI-13 all about the race course."

"He still has reservations," I said after a pause. "He might consider lending his name if the race were fae only, and if Mr Rustle were to oversee the organisation of the race and all its regulations."

"Oh, good show, my dear," said Sir Reginald. "You're more skilled than I am at this negotiation business."

"He said that?" Yardley didn't look like he believed me.

"Would you like me to get my aunt Rose and her spectacles to vouch for his approval? I see her with the inspector."

"Ah... no. That won't be necessary," the mayor said. His face had drained of colour. "I will consider Sir Reginald's proposal and meet with the racing council about the matter."

With that, he turned and strode off, waving at another guest.

"His idea has merit," Sir Reginald said. "But he takes it much too far. What is that American saying? Above my corpse?"

"Over my dead body," I said. "Meaning they'd have to kill us to get what they want."

"I'm afraid that might have already happened."

❧ 18 ❧

Elain returned, empty-handed. Aunt Rose and Io trailed her. I expected to see a ginger cat dangling from Elain's clenched fist.

"What did you do with Punkin?"

"Gave him to the Bobbies," Elain said.

Io chuckled. Aunt Rose smiled.

"Go get him, dearie," she said. "He'll have been properly scared enough for one fortnight."

"This party looks to be winding down," I said, then looked at Elain. "Show me where?"

We drifted through what remained of the guests. A handful still stood with the lieutenant colonel. Wait staff with high-lighted hair moved through the room, collecting left-behind champagne flutes and other glassware. Even though they weren't the normal colourful streaks, I could recognise their nature. Even the males had the highlights. Pixies seemed to fit into the service industry. Their friendly and outgoing nature, along with their energetic demeanour, kept them moving through the ball-room. Discarded glasses were retrieved almost before they touched the tables.

One pixie girl, Rachel from Barti Ddu's pub, dressed in a smart black top and matching slacks, hurried to open the door to the corridor for us. A small crowd gathered at the bottom of the stairs, including the uniformed green orcish fellows I had last seen when Sir Reginald's demon escaped.

"Mother had the inspector bring the Bobbies in to check each guest on the way out." We walked side by side down the grand staircase, into the dimly lit main hall. "No one will be allowed to drive out until they're sober and it's daylight. Mother doesn't want to lose another guest."

A couple in nice attire stood by a green and golden disc set in front of the door. A small fellow in a green suit held his wand at the ready.

"Teleport discs," Elain said. "Oh... a Yardley tiff going on. Let's stay back so we don't intrude."

"You mean spy on them," I whispered.

"Of course. It's what I do."

"I don't see why you won't come home," Gemma de Yardley said. She stood with hands on hips. Her outfit was more gown than dress, and she was at the upper end of formal for this event. Silver jewellery hung from both ears, cascading around her neck. She brandished her index finger at the man in front of her. "You are never home, Yerdleh," she groused. "Always off working deals. I want some attention too."

"The race, dearest," Mayor Yardley said. "I need to speak to Mr Calhoun one more time. He's ready to flip and go against that Australian. I need his vote on the commission tomorrow. I believe I've secured the other two mundane votes. I need Calhoun to get the tie, and, if there is a tie, his vote counts twice as chair. I've hung my reputation on getting that race into the valley. I can't let this opportunity pass me by."

"Oh, pooh on racing," his wife declared, rolling her eyes.

"Why did I ever marry you?" She waved at the leprechaun at the teleport disc. "Get me away from him. NOW!"

With a pop, she disappeared.

"Why did you marry me? For the size of my trust fund, obviously," he said to the sizzle of static that remained after Gemma was zapped away. "Oh, good evening, ladies. Just sending my wife home. Have you seen that fellow from Texas?"

"I believe he's in the upstairs lounge with the Australian racers," Elain said. "Top of the stairs, turn right, third door towards the front. Avoid the second door. That's my brother's weapons room. It's got all sorts of alarms if anyone sets foot in there. With my brother's ideas of punishment for intruders, you're far safer if you avoid it completely."

"Diolch. Excuse me, please."

He hurried off.

I cast an eye at the small fae in the green suit.

"Ah... the leprechaun teleport crystals?"

"Yes, Mother required teleporting for anyone who wants to leave tonight. All drivers have to stay."

"Why wouldn't they just teleport in and avoid the hassle?"

"Well, first you have the racers," Elain said. "They love to drive, and they won't accept otherwise. So they will spend the night in the guest wing. Mother had some witches from London come in and magic up some sleep cubes. Mini hotel rooms. She's hoping that enough of the guests leave that we won't have to stage any in the ballroom. We'd like to lock the doors to that room and leave the trophies and such until tomorrow. The staff has worked enough this week."

Elain led me to an orc who looked familiar.

"Robert 34-764," she called. One of the dark-skinned Bobbies turned. "I'd like to retrieve my detainee."

"As you wish, Agent E-487," the Bobbie captain replied. "Lady Ebrel," he said with a tip of his helmet to me. "Your familiar seems bladdered this evening. We've taken some of the spark out of his tail."

"Oh! I may need to learn how to do that."

"He's quite the handful. Right this way."

Punkin lay curled in the back of a stainless steel cage. Nothing else was in there. He shivered when Robert 34-whatever unlocked the cage door.

"No more, please!"

"Serves you right," I said. "What did he do this time?"

"He ate through my last bag of Emerald Golden from Colombia. It was open, and he was rolling in the beans. He's been sick once already."

"Are those the beans they grow at high altitudes? About one hundred dollars a bag?"

"Oh, yes. I'm not worried about the money," she said with a wink at me. "But your familiar has expensive tastes for a drunk."

"Make them stoooop!" Punkin wailed and shivered in my arms. He smelled of lavender and damp fur.

"What did you do to him?" I couldn't repress a chuckle. He was so pathetic. I imagined many probes and kitty-sized handcuffs.

"My lads gave him a right smart bath," Robert said. "Good thing Her Grace wasn't here. She'd have had him shaved."

"No!" Punkin cried and tried to curl even tighter into a ball. "Not her. That woman has no limits."

"I wouldn't recommend teleporting anywhere," the Bobbie captain said. "With as much as he's under the influence of, he's likely to turn himself inside out with that much magic."

"Oh, great. So what am I going to do with him?"

"You can stay here tonight," Elain said. "You can have the spare room in my flat. We'll give him a bed in my kitchen. That way, if he's sick again, it will be easy to clean."

We stopped by Macsen's study on the way to Elain's rooms.

"Do you want me to keep the coffee bar closed in the morning?" Aunt Rose asked when we told her my plans.

"I can drive you down in the morning," Elain said. "I promise, my demon isn't as grumpy as Io's new one."

Punkin had stopped shivering but was still curled in my arms.

"Are they gone?" He had one eye half open.

"The Bobbies are still here, Fuzzbutt," I said. "Any more shenanigans, and I'll let them have you again."

"Meh... they don't scare me," he said and dozed off again.

"Come if you can, dearie," Aunt Rose said. "If not, I'll have the pixies only make regular coffee." She stood and started looking around.

"Your purse is on your arm, and your spectacles are on your head," Rhian said.

"Oh, diolch, dear. I'd forget me head if it weren't on my shoulders."

AN HOUR LATER, ELAIN AND I SAT IN HER APARTMENT. WE had each changed back into comfy clothes. I didn't ask if Elain was still packing whatever assassin and spy gear she normally carried. Punkin was curled on a towel wrapped around a fluffy pillow in her kitchen.

"How can a cat snore that loud?" I asked, looking at him in amazement.

"Well," she said, "he's not exactly a cat."

"Still, that is loud. Even Jake didn't snore like that. Punkin is as noisy as Jake's bike was."

"Um... April?" Jake said from near the door. His tone of voice said he knew he wasn't supposed to be in here.

"This better be good, Jake."

"Or bad," he said and pulled another ghost into the room.

My chin dropped.

"What?" said Elain. "Ebrel? What's wrong?"

"I'm sorry, mate," Bryce Rustle's ghost said. "I have no idea what happened. This young man said I needed to come see you."

19

E
lain and I charged down the hall. Elain had her phone
out for a second or two. Just long enough to say, "Code
18, ballroom."

I felt a surge of magic. The castle rumbled as though the
drawbridge had been raised, and the gates closed.

"Magic protection," she said. "No one in or out."

I almost ran Neirin over as I rounded the last corner.

He raised a finger to his lips. His other hand held not a wand,
but one of his throwing knives. This one had a green magical
shimmer. A finger flicked towards the other set of double doors.
Elain nodded, and she pulled me towards them.

"Wand out," she whispered and drew her own. "Don't blast
anything that looks like Neirin or I. Only shoot if we go
down."

She put one hand on the door latch, the other raised. Three
fingers raised, then two, then one. She and Neirin both eased the
doors open. Her hand dipped into her sweater and pulled out a
knife to match Neirin's. The glitter of green enchantment
sparkled for a second before fading. She and her brother slipped

inside. More magic, and balls of light streaked towards the high ceiling.

Behind me, footsteps pounded on the stairs.

"What is going on?" Inspector Owain asked. One of the Roberts was with him. I didn't look long enough to note which number was on his vest.

"Clear," Neirin called. "Come in." He and Elain both had their hands back inside their coats. No knives in sight.

Before us, in front of the table with Sir Reginald's cricket gear, lay Bryce Rustle's body.

"Those are professional knives," Owain said, looking at the body. "The type you throw."

"Those are my knives," Neirin said. "The question is: how did someone got them out of the weapons hall without setting off my alarms?"

"Crikey!" Rustle's ghost said. "I am dead."

"I told you, mate," Jake said.

"Oh, hello, Bryce," Reg said, appearing in the room. "Someone did you in too?"

Bryce's ghost shook his head. "How...? The last thing I remember is wandering off to find the loo."

"I thought I smelled blood," Macsen said. He and Rhian entered the ballroom. "Son, why are your knives in Mr Rustle?"

"We're trying to figure that out, Father," Neirin said. His normal jovial attitude was gone. His eyes, when they swept the room, had gone hard. Very hard. No more games with him. Elain had the same look. Neither of them were still. They were on the prowl and moved to every nook and cranny in the room.

"How many Bobbies are still here?" The inspector had a hard edge to his voice, and his wand was in hand.

"Full crew still. We were just beginning to pack up," the Bobby said. "Evening, Lady Ebrel. How's your familiar?" This evidently was the captain I had met before. He hadn't shifted attitudes. From what I could tell, the Bobbies were always on edge.

"Sleeping, unlike Mr Rustle."

"I can't believe I'm dead." Bryce sounded bewildered. Sir Reginald put a ghostly hand on Rustle's spectral shoulder.

"Death amnesia, old man. It takes several months to wear off."

"Crikey, I need a beer," Rustle said.

"Sorry, mate," Jake said. "They go right through us and have no taste at all."

I chuckled at that. Everyone looked at me.

"Sorry," I said. "The ghosts are trying to get Bryce acclimated to his new condition."

"Is he here?" Owain fished for his notebook in a jacket pocket. "I left the goggles out in my car. I'll need you to interpret again."

"He says he went to find the loo but can't remember anything about coming in here." I shrugged. "The ghost of Sir Reginald said it's death amnesia."

"Lasts for several months," Jake said.

"I remember you mentioning that before," Owain said. He turned towards the Bobby captain. "Get your men in here for a full crime-scene analysis."

"Understood," he said and raised his arms. "Everyone not in uniform or dead... that includes the undead, please exit the room. Follow Inspector Jones for debriefing." He toggled the microphone on his vest. "Robert 678-347, bring a full forensics kit and any available personnel to my location... Affirmative... Full lockdown still in effect."

An hour later, I was back in Macsen's study, sitting across from Rhian and Lord Edeirnion. Elain sat next to me.

"Hey, there's a dead Australian in the ballroom," Punkin announced as he pushed open the door. "And a bunch of

Bobbies. I'd wager one of them did him in. Probably the ones who hosed me down with that cold water."

"You deserved it," I said. "If you're going to get drunk on coffee beans, would you at least go for the cheap ones?"

"Stay out of my personal supply," Elain said, her voice cold. A knife that hadn't been there before was in her hand. She flipped it a full rotation and caught it again. And again.

"Point taken," Punkin said. "Women sure get mean about their coffee."

"Hey!"

"Yes, you are stuck with me," he said. "Only 36,522 more days to go."

"That sounds like a jail sentence," Elain said. "At least he's keeping track of it for you."

"Did Jake or Sir Reginald notice anything?" Rhian asked. Owain had already questioned me about this.

"Nothing," I said. "Jake found him wandering around dazed. He had a snoop... around... Sorry, what do you call it?"

"A nose-about," Macsen added. "A very British term for having a... look-see? Is that the term you Americans use?"

"Close enough. Americans don't have the way with language that Brits do. After Jake realised what happened, he brought Bryce to me. Once he described the ballroom, Elain was out the door with her phone in hand."

"Training," was all she said.

"Neirin was fast," I said with a glance at my friend. "He was there before we were."

"His flat is closer, almost right across the hall. Next to that is the weapons room."

"The inspector seemed surprised at that," I said. "Your brother could be in for a rough night of questions."

"He's done worse to me," she said. I raised an eyebrow.

"Training. You don't get be our level at MI-13 and not face time in abuse-training situations."

"I'm positive I don't want to know about that," I said and wrapped my arms around my chest. Abuse training didn't sound like they taught her to be abusive, rather how to survive it.

"Your instincts serve you well," Elain said, then fixed her gaze on Punkin. "However, I'm happy to use some of those techniques if I find a Fuzzbum in my coffee again."

"Have you tried what most British call coffee?" he said, then stood and stretched. "Instant coffee crystals. Blech! That freeze-dried taste makes my tongue go numb."

"Why did instant coffee stay popular over here?" I asked.

"The war, my dear," the lieutenant colonel said, wandering into the room. "After the Second War to End All Wars, when you Yanks had brought us that most vile of crystallised substances—instant coffee for the lads off fighting—too many of our countrymen and women had gotten used to it. Quicker and easier than putting on a kettle for a proper cuppa." He reached into several pockets on his brown tweed jacket again. No large-barrelled elephant musket this time. He eventually pulled out a pipe.

"Don't worry, my dear," he said. "This one is magical. You'll not smell a whiff. Unless you'd like one of your own? I might have another tucked in here." He clenched his pipe between his teeth and started rummaging in his coat pockets again.

"Ah!" He pulled another pipe forth. I shook my head. "Ladies? Macsen?"

"Perhaps later," Elain's father said and raised his glass of crimson liquid. "This varietal doesn't go well with a smoke."

"That your son I saw heading in to talk with the inspector?"

"Yes," Macsen said. "Bryce Rustle was found with two of Neirin's knives in his back. Lady Ebrel says his ghost doesn't remember enough to give the inspector and the Bobbies anything to go on."

"Your son is very skilled with weapons." He took a long draw from his pipe. I could see the red glow in its bowl, but no smoke drifted out, nor did he exhale any.

He noticed me watching. "As I said, magic pipe. No smoke, miss. Did I ever tell you about the time young Neirin helped us with the rakshasa?"

"What is that?"

"A demonic champion, found in North Africa, the Middle East, and East Asia. They're partial to desert and scrubland," he said. "Looks like a tiger. A well-dressed, bipedal tiger. Smart, cagey, and powerful with magic. Bernard and I were tasked with drawing it out of the protections it had woven around itself in the desert. This one was very skilled. Still, we had a delightful time with the ladies in his harem. There was this one lass—"

"Rhodri!" Rhian said. "Let's not shock Ebrel with your more colourful exploits this early. She's barely gotten to meet you."

"Three days ago, I didn't even know fae existed," I said. "It's okay. A story about a tiger demon sounds so much more interesting than what the inspector is doing to Neirin."

"Well, Bernard snuck in under the flap of the tent once we finished our tea time with the ladies. Stole something the chap was sure to want returned, so he'd chase after us. Bernard was skilled at transformations, especially of himself. Could always change into whatever kind of animal we needed. He even swam as a seal with a few selkies once."

"A selkie? Like Sir Reginald's mother?"

"No, no, not like her. It was her. Bernard noticed her when we were going after those old sea hags. The selkies in that pod of seals gave us the information we needed to find the old witches. There was a human girl with their pod one moment, then an extra seal the next. Much prettier than the sea hags we were trying to locate."

"What is a sea hag?"

"An evil witch," he said. "Someone who has invested so much of their soul into the dark side of the arts they have no inner beauty left. The coven we were tracking was of three of such fearsome creatures. Three sea fae that had turned to evil. Again, Bernard snuck in as a local seal, found the cave where they were bubbling up their cauldron of vile poison, ready to destroy the life in the sea, draining it of energy to fuel their magic. He snuck the explosive crystals into their pile of fire fuel, and we retreated. Unfortunately, a hag grabbed it right off and threw on their fire before we were far enough to avoid the blast."

"You were injured?" I asked.

"I now see better out of my left ear than my eye," he said. "That was powerful magic they were cooking."

"What happened to the hags?"

"Destroyed," he said. "On the way back, we had Davy Jones search for that pod of seals with the selkie family.

"The Davy Jones?" I asked incredulously.

"Of course."

"You got to hang out with the lead singer of the Monkees?"

"He means the pirate," Elain said, snickering. "You know... Davy Jones's Locker."

"We found the pod again. The selkies were, however, in human form," the lieutenant colonel said. "Bernard had an eye for that lass he saw swimming with them on the way out."

"He had a crush on a seal?" I was confused.

"On the selkie, the shapeshifter." The colonel chuckled. "She seemed to like Bernard as well. Charming fellow when he tried to be. But her father had other ideas about whom she should marry. He was pod chief and kept a tight watch on Bernard after that. The lass tried to leave her seal skin out where Bernard could grab it. Then she'd have to marry him. Without it, she couldn't change into seal form. Check and mate, so to speak, against her father."

"I had a similar issue with my own father about my marriage," Rhian added. "Becoming a vampire wasn't reversible, so he acquiesced."

"Bernard convinced me," the colonel said, "to help him steal the seal skin while he distracted her father. Her only condition was that she be allowed to return to her pod when their first child reached five years of age. Bernard agreed. Poor man would have none other than she. I could see it in his face."

"You said they had disagreements?"

"After the marriage," Rhian added, "Bernard discovered she had a fiery temper. He got more woman than he realized. We think that caused the great conflagration in Swansea."

"Why did they fight?"

"I'm not sure," Rhodri said. "I suspect he had second thoughts and refused to give back the skin. She was a quiet soul until you crossed her. I'd heard many a diatribe from their home. That was one forceful woman when crossed."

"So what happened with the tiger demon?" I remembered that we had gotten sidetracked on Bernard's marriage instead of the demonic problems. "Reg's car had a demon try to escape after someone drilled holes through the surrounding spells."

"The cauldron," Elain said. "I see where you're going with this."

"Hmm..." Rhodri took another pull on his pipe. Again no smoke issued from it, nor from him. "The old chap has likely reformed his body by now. Demons don't die. They just go back to whichever part of Hades they're from and spend years reforming. Though the damage Neirin, Bernard, and I did to it may be enough to force it into a longer recovery. Bernard reckoned about a century."

"When did you face this rashaker?"

"Rakshasa," the lieutenant colonel said. "About a century ago. Well, before young Elain joined our merry band of mischief and mayhem."

"So he might have reformed by now? And be coming after Bernard's son?" I rubbed my temples. "This talk of magic and demons is making my head ache."

The lieutenant colonel held the pipe out and stared at it for several seconds. "I can see your point, my dear. That old tiger chappie may just want his pipe back."

❧ 2 0 ❧

I stumbled out of Elain's spare bed in time for a quick shower. She hopped into the bath right after me, so I whipped up two macchiatos on her home-brew espresso machine while I waited.

"Brit laws. Although we can have beverages in our cars, the laws are loose enough to give the constables room to fine you for drinking from a cup instead of driving. Best not to get into the habit of taking a cup with you," she said and tried to drink hers fast. The first sip was still too hot, though. One wand wave later, she could take longer sips.

"Magic comes in handy," I said and kicked the pillow Punkin was dozing on. "Move it, Fuzzbutt, or you're walking down the mountain."

He eyed our coffees as he stretched. "Did you make me one?"

"Not after your shenanigans last night," I said. "I wanted to try that special roast she had. Now there is cat slobber covering what you didn't eat. Blech!"

He showed me his butt in response as he headed outside.

Elain drove fast, but at least her demon wasn't trying to kill us on the trip down. I didn't have to clench the door handle on the winding road down to Misty Valley. I even had the ability to call ahead and tell Nia to power on the espresso machine and get it warming.

We made good time and rolled into the carpark next to the café without incident. The timed lock on the front door to Mystic Brews clicked when we approached.

"Ebrel!" Nia called when I walked in. "Rose wouldn't let me turn your machine on until you called. Can you make us tornados? Mia's sluggish like a human this morning."

"When you take your break," I said. "Drink coffee with some syrup if you need the buzz. Guests come first."

"Mmm.... Rose's scones," Elain said, sniffing the air. "And her clotted cream is always fresh."

"Your parents are vamps," I said. Fortunately, no clients were in so far. "With their diet, hearing clotted next to cream doesn't sound appetising."

"Oh, good, dearie, you made it," Aunt Rose said, coming out of the kitchen. She handed a plate to Elain with a cream-covered scone. "Thanks for taking care of me niece, sweetie. On the house."

"You're the best, Rhosyn," Elain said. She took a seat at a table close to the coffee bar. I got busy prepping my workstation.

"Clotted cream," Elain said, "is full-fat milk heated then allowed to cool in shallow pans."

She took a bite and rolled her head back, chewing slowly. "Mmm... this makes up for Fuzzbum getting into my coffee."

"But clotted?"

"When the milk cools, dearie," Aunt Rose added, "the cream gels together. It is much creamier, though courser than the cream you use in coffee."

Elain leaned across the glass shield at my espresso machine.

"Try," she said, holding her fork out with a hunk of cream-covered scone on it.

"Oh..." I said after I ate it. "If this sensation is anything like what the pixies get from the caramel macchiatos, I can see why they're addicted."

"Please tell me there is coffee in here," Mayor Yardley called from the door. He sounded like a man who had just come in from the desert, seeking his first drink of water in a week.

"What will it be, Mr Mayor?" Nia held her order pad in hand.

"The largest coffee you have," he said. His eyes were bloodshot, his clothing rumpled. I recognised it as what he had worn to the wake last evening. "Which has more of a kick? Dark or light roast?"

"Light or medium," I said. "Though the dark I get is a medium-dark. It still has a kick."

"I need the caffeine," he added. "Add whatever you need to give me a wake-up. I feel so un-British not taking tea."

I pulled a double shot of espresso and dumped it into a large ceramic mug, then topped it off with medium roast. He tapped his wand on the payment pad without even looking at what Nia rang up. Then he waved his wand above the cup, and the steam diminished under his cooling spell. He drank like a man from the desert. A moment later, he set the cup on the counter.

"Another. Just like that."

"How about one with just coffee?" I suggested. "Or you'll be as jittery as Punkin. Have a seat and tell us what happened."

"Bryce Rustle happened!" He plopped into the chair by Elain and eyed the last bite of her scone. She had that hard glint in her eye. The fork made a slow journey to her mouth, her eyes locked on Yardley. I kept waiting for the soundtrack of a Spaghetti Western movie to begin playing. Showdown at the Clotted Cream Corral. Yerdleh Yardley didn't stand a chance against Elain and her quick-draw fork.

He blinked, then slumped.

"That fool got himself killed, and Inspector Jones believes I had something to do with the murder. There are Bobbies all over Castle Raven now. Had one standing guard in the ballroom even after they took Rustle's body away."

"Well, he probably had a good reason to kill me," Bryce said from the back table. He and Sir Reginald faded in. Distance didn't seem to matter to them. "With my seat on the racing commission empty, the votes are split about Yerd-face's race. Two of the humans are leaning towards it. Macsen and Rhodri against. That leaves it to Calhoun to decide."

Elain watched me and had her head cocked. I gave a minor nod to let her know I was getting information from someone she could neither see nor hear.

"What happens now that Bryce is gone?" I asked. The morning was quiet so far. With most of the village still at the Castle or sleeping off their partying, we had an hour before the café got busy.

"How should I know?" Yardley said. "I'm not on the commission. They'll deadlock... oh!"

"Oh, what?" Elain asked.

"Calhoun, the mundane, he'll get the tie-breaker vote."

"Wish I could remember what happened last night," Bryce's ghost said. "Yerd-bum is the type I'd expect to knife me."

Jake appeared behind him in time to hear the accusation.

"I see why the inspector was interested in you," I remarked. "Where were you when Bryce was killed?"

"Um... well... I, uh..."

"That's not a very good alibi," Elain said. "The Bobbies said there were no prints on the murder weapons."

"Not true," Yardley said. "The only prints were those of your brother. The inspector told me that much."

"They are his knives," Elain said. She scooted the empty

scone plate away from her and crossed her arms across her chest. One hand dipped into her jacket. The mayor seemed oblivious to her professional-agent tone and demeanour. "Of course his prints would be on them," she continued. "Someone needed to use them in a way that didn't leave prints on them. Someone good at moving things and not touching them."

"Not you too," Yardley said, closing his eyes and leaning on the table, head in his hands. "You might as well ask my wife. She's as good with her wand as I am. I tried to get her to help me with a stage show years ago. Performance is beneath a de Umple!"

"Why would she do in Bryce?" Elain's tone was still hard, cold.

"You didn't see her chasing after him last evening? Rustle gave her the cold shoulder in a very Aussie way. No one can deliver a hard slam like an Australian. She'd never been ignored that way by a man." He took a large swig from his second coffee and looked at me. "That's good. Why doesn't my coffee taste this good?"

"You probably buy the instant crystals," I said. "I'm here to get you Brits to change your ways."

"Hah! Good luck with my wife. Gemma only drinks proper English teas. And chases after only proper English gentlemen. And Australians. And anyone else that she believes will worship her because she's a de Umple."

Behind Sir Reginald and Bryce, Jake plucked two of the larger feathers off his coat and tossed them like knives at Yardley's back. They flew straight but faded before they reached the mayor's slumped shoulders.

Something buzzed. The mayor pulled his phone from the inner pocket of his rumpled jacket. "Excuse me, please," he said and rose. His thumbs glided across the screen, tapping out a message. He paused to drain the last of his coffee and waved the empty cup my way.

"Much appreciated, miss."

"Come back when you're not so tired," I said. "I plan on having some tastings in the next few weeks, to help everyone learn how good coffee can actually taste."

"Perhaps," he said. "I've got get through the commission meeting before I can think past tonight." He pulled the door open, still typing on his phone.

Jake followed Yardley out. Every few steps, he plucked a ghostly feather from his coat and flung it, like he was throwing one of Neirin's knives, at the mayor's back. One feather turned solid and fluttered to the floor right as the door shut behind the mayor. Jake phased through the door, following.

I chuckled and retrieved the feather before another guest came in. Didn't want a health violation because of it on the floor.

Tourists began arriving, and I had a busy morning. Nia was correct that her sister was slow this morning. That was unusual for the energetic pixies. I snuck her a caramel macchiato and sent her on her break early. The macchiato had extra caramel since she looked like she needed the sugar.

Elain hung out at the café until the door locked after the morning crowd. The nice thing about our café was that Aunt Rose didn't want to deal with a lunch or dinner. She only worried about mornings and tea time.

"Were you serious about coffee tastings?" Elain asked while I cleaned up the espresso bar.

"Of course. I wanted to wait until I got my roaster and could get it dialled in. However, I could start with some simpler roasts. From what I've seen, the British palate needs to be trained for good coffee."

"Oh, that would be wonderful," she said. "One of the few

problems with a family like mine is lack of a shared meal time. I'd love for mother to try some coffees."

"It's not the right varietal, correct...?"

"She claims to have a well-defined palate," Elain said. "Her beverage isn't one I want to try. And that's the only beverage she can have. Something about vamps means only blood, no other food or drink. That's why mother pulls the pixies in whenever she entertains. Jonathan is enough for kitchen staff since I'm the only resident who eats real food. He only has to cook for routine guests like the lieutenant colonel."

"You don't want to be a vamp?"

She shook her head, then shrugged. "Fae live long lives. Vamps are practically immortal. To get that benefit, however, you have to die first. That's how Father saved Neirin."

"I didn't catch all of that earlier. What was that about Neirin almost dying, then becoming a vamp?"

"A couple centuries ago, Father was leading troops in a night raid during some war in Spain. He was quite the military man. He and the lieutenant colonel spent some time together before Father retired. That's when the Queen's Company tapped Rhodri for special missions and teamed him up with Bernard Dewsberry."

"Back to Neirin? Did they exchange blood?" I was trying to remember my vampire lore from all the old horror movies.

"Something like that," Elain said. "Anyway, Neirin was dying. Father had taken him in as an adjunct and was training him to take command. He says Neirin was already like a son to him. I know the details of the bloodletting and drinking. It's not a topic for polite company."

"Sounds... um... interesting?"

"Just don't ask my brother about it. He's such a flirt, and will do his best to make you feel as though he's seducing you with the offer of immortality." She tapped her finger on her lips. "He actually did that to Yerdleh's wife before they married. The poor woman wanted so much to be loved and didn't see my brother for the non-serious flirt that he was. She was right put out that he wouldn't give her the blood gift and bring her into the family."

"Not nice to lead her on," I said.

"One of his few mistakes," she admitted. "He'll flirt. Gemma's experience showed him he needs to judge character better. You're strong enough that he can keep playing the love-struck fool for ages."

"Are fae always so complicated?"

"In dating? Of course," Elain said.

"Be careful of the pixie lads," Nia said. Her sister nodded behind her. "They like to go after the tall fae. A few of the pixie guys went after Gemma and learned fast how demanding she is. She's got a reputation now, and only the naïve ones give her any attention. Or Dewi. We've warned him about her. He only chases you tall girls."

"Tall?"

"That's what we call you human-based fae," Mia said. "We get tired out if we stay in our human forms too long. That's why Rose closes for the afternoon. We can shift back and rest up for being big in the afternoon."

"I saw a lot of staff at the wake," I said. "There were some nice-looking male waiters. And female ones. Were they all pixies?"

"Yes. They had glamours to hide their nature," Mia said. "I was bartending. You never made it out to my area. I was in the lounge with the Australian racers. But since some mundane humans were at the event, we had to hide our nature. It was a downright shame what happened to Mr Rustle. Those Bobbies put the scare into us with their questioning. It's a wonder I made it back here in time to work."

"Did you notice anything off that night?" Elain asked. "Anyone sneaking around?"

Mia shrugged. "The mayor was in with the Aussies. He kept trying to talk to those three humans. He liked to show off and kept trying to get me and the other girl working the bar to shift into our other forms. Even tried to get Sari to take a walk with one of them."

"He was trying to hook pixies up with human dignitaries? I will... urrrgh!" Elain clenched her hands, then took a deep breath. "I'm sorry. What happened after?"

"Rachel heard and told him to back off. She's the afternoon staff at Barti Ddu's. She was our shift lead that night."

"Good for her. Anything else?"

"No... well, when I went on break and wandered off to find the loo, Mrs Yardley was in there checking her hair when I went in. I hoped she didn't go into the Aussie room, not with the way her husband was acting. On my way back," Mia continued, "one door stood ajar in the main hallway. It wasn't my house, and it wasn't an area we were told to staff."

"Which door?"

"Second door to the right of the stairs," Mia said. "The one right next to the lounge with the Aussies."

Elain glanced at me, worry in her eyes. I remembered her giving directions to the mayor that night and told him to avoid that room. It was the room where Neirin kept his weapons.

"When was that?"

"I'm not sure," Mia said, "but the lockdown started maybe half an hour after I got back from the loo."

❧ 21 ❧

I slid into a chair once my station was clean. Punkin had his head in the cupboard, counting the inventory.

"Slow day," he called. "Only need a bag of each. I can take an early nap."

"Wait until my roaster comes in," I called. "You'll be magicking beans into bags every afternoon. No napping."

"And no eating the beans," Elain called.

"He better not! That's our profit."

"Did you catch that Gemma Yardley returned to the wake after we saw her leave?" Elain said.

"What? Oh! Good catch." I hadn't noticed the timing when Mia told us. "Why would she come back?"

Elain shrugged. "She wanted to go slap Bryce for ignoring her?"

"I didn't ignore her," Bryce said from the table where he and Sir Reginald had sat all morning. It was a slow morning in the café, so no one had sat at that table. "When Mrs Yardley decided I needed to be her personal champion and tell her she was a good-looking Sheila, I shut her down. I don't need that kind of woman in my life."

"Are you married?" I asked.

"No," he said. "There are a few ladies I like to spend time with, however, we all like our freedom. Guess I'm freer now."

I passed the conversation on to Elain.

"Did he see Gemma again after that?"

"Not at all," he said. "She avoided me like a mouse hiding from a snake."

Elain rose. "Want to go have a chat with Gemma?"

"Why not?" I said. "She and her husband are both up to something... I'm not sure if it's the same thing, though."

We walked, since the grey skies were clearing. Elain headed out to the valley, not deeper into the village.

"The Yardleys have a nice estate at the edge of town," she said. "Fancy homes out here. Some development going on. The bed-and-breakfasts who will take mundanes are out another mile or two. We like to keep our evenings fae only."

We had lost the pavement, or sidewalks, a few hundred yards before, and had to walk in the road. Elain jerked me to the side as we crested a hill. A silver Jaguar barrelled past us, leaving a stench of brimstone.

"And there she goes," Elain said. "At least, I think Gemma was at the wheel. The mayor's wife drives faster than most of us can get away with."

"Time to turn back," I said. "At least we got a nice walk in."

"Let's keep going. I want to have a nose-about at stately Yardley Manor."

"You sound like TV presenter reading the script for a daily soap opera intro."

"Oh, I know. Don't tell anyone I watch them. I'm so pathetic. MI-13 agent, one of the Deadly Duo, most talked about agents after Bernard and Rhodri, and I still have to catch my stories on the tele."

The hedges to the side of the road opened to a gated yard. A handsome pixie man was waving his wand and trimming the topiaries near the front gate. Several of the shaped bushes stood about the lawn. I spied several imaginary creatures, like a dragon, a unicorn, and a troll in the menagerie.

"Dewi, you shouldn't be using your wand this close to the road," Elain scolded him. "And put a shirt on."

"Gemma likes me without my shirt," he said, turning to lean on the iron gate. "Oh, Lady Ebrel. The girls are talking about your tornados. I might have to come try one."

I could understand why Gemma liked him without his shirt. He was definitely eye candy. Sleek and toned. His hair was blond with greenish highlights. His green eyes sparkled.

"Keep to yourself, Dewi," Elain said. "Ebrel's been warned off the pixie guys."

"She won't know what she's missing," he said and winked at me. "As to your earlier accusation, the wards on the road told me fae were coming up, so I didn't worry about using my wand. My gardening wand turns red when a non-fae is approaching.

"So you left your shirt off just for us?" I said. "You really didn't have to."

"I wanted to make sure you appreciated the sights here in our little valley."

He was even more annoying than Mayor Yardley. I could understand why Mia and Nia warned me off of the pixie males.

"Where did your boss go in such a hurry?" Elain asked. "We didn't get to chat last night at the wake."

"Her mum's estate." Dewi shrugged. "She's wound up at Mr Yardley. Sure he's up to something."

"Is that why she snuck back to the wake last night?"

Elain shot me a look, but Dewi didn't notice. He was too

busy leaning on the fence for me. He kept shifting his weight ever so slightly. Enough to accent another set of muscles.

"I figured she'd be back, and I had her bath drawn." He shrugged again, which allowed him to shift and lean on his other arm. More flexing. It was getting comical. "She came back, changed into more casual clothing. Well, casual for a de Umple. All dark colours. She only put on onyx jewellery. And her black trainers. A few moments later, I heard the pop of the teleport pad."

"You've got your own pad here?" Elain sounded surprised.

"Gemma had it installed in her suite," Dewi said. "An expensive one too. She can get to any other unlocked pad." Another shrug, followed by a gleaming smile as he rippled his muscles again. "The mayor isn't aware she has it. I figured she'd use it to get to her mother's. She took the Jag this time."

"Suitcase with her?"

"Oh, never," he said. "She maintains a complete wardrobe at her family estate. She always travels light. Care to come in and experience more of the landscaping? I've got some in the back that I'm especially proud of."

"I'm sure you are," Elain said. "Perhaps I'll ask Nia to come down and take a look."

"Um... we stopped dating a year ago when I took this position."

"I wonder why?" Elain said. "Go flex in front of the mirror, Dewi. Leave the tall girls alone."

"Gemma likes me," he said, standing back to his full height. "You don't know what you're missing."

"And we're grateful," Elain said, taking my arm and pulling me back towards the village.

"Yuck. I feel like I need a shower," I said a moment later. "Are all pixie guys like him?"

"No, there are better ones. But Dewi is one of the worst. I'd rather subject you to my brother for a few days than five minutes with Dewi." She shivered. "He's just creepy. But he is exactly the type of admirer Gemma craves."

"What are you out here for?" Jake asked, floating beside me.

"Wanted to talk to the mayor's wife, Jake." I said his name so Elain would know he was here. "Where have you been?"

"Around. Reg and Bryce were heading to a race in France. I don't understand French. Still, it was fun watching the cars. Even more fun now that I realised I can sit on them when they run." He stood like a fancy hood ornament, frozen in a running pose.

I passed that on to Elain with a description of his antics. She laughed.

"Why are you back here?"

"Bryce said I should come back and tell you what the mayor did when he left."

"Which was...?" Grrr! Jake had a way of not sharing what he knew he should.

"Oh, Yerd-bum... I love how Bryce makes up names for people. He calls you—"

"Don't! I do not want to know."

"Coffee Sheila," Jake told me anyway. He nodded towards Elain. "She's Lady Sneak."

I laughed and shared with Elain.

"Well, at least they're accurate names."

"What did Mayor Yardley do?"

"Oh, he just sent a message on his phone."

"To whom?" Jake was being annoying and didn't realise it.

"Someone named R. No other name. The text read that he wanted to meet R before the big race meeting today."

"R? Like Rhodri?" Elain said. "I don't trust him to not ambush him."

"Dang it! Jake, why didn't you tell me before?"

"I didn't know it was important." He sounded perplexed.

"Bryce and Reg said I had to get back here and tell you. We ghosts can't do anything about it."

"Come on!" Elain started jogged back to the car. "Rhodri and my father are the only two fae left on the racing commission. I don't trust Yardley to not try to harm one of them."

✲ 2 2 ✲

Punkin ran out and jumped in the car with Elain and I.

"What's the rush?"

"Gemma and the mayor are both off somewhere, right as the race commission meeting is about to begin." I was still fighting to get my seatbelt buckled when Elain backed the car out of its space. I grabbed the door handle as she punched the accelerator.

"You trying to drive like Io or like Gemma?"

"I'm as good as Io," she said. "I could probably take on Bryce and Sir Reginald. The training at MI-13 EVOP is great fun. I always take a refresher each year for the thrill."

"What's an Evob?"

"EVOP," she said. I tightened my grip on the handle. "Enchanted Vehicle Ordinance and Pursuit. Humans have a slightly different name with 'avoidance' in the acronym. MI-13 is more concerned about taking out the bad guys than avoiding accidents."

"You said 'ordinance.' Is this thing armed?"

"Hmmm... that sounds like a question I'd have to direct up to the official inquiry administration office. Their forms to submit questions are very, very long."

She thumbed a button on her steering wheel.

"Call Neirin," Elain pronounced.

The sound of the phone buzzing rang out on the car's speakers and went unanswered at the other end.

"Disconnect. Call Mother."

"Hello, sweetie," Rhian's voice drifted out. "What are you doing?"

"Bringing Ebrel to the caer," Elain said. "Tried to get Neirin. No answer."

"He's down with MI-5. Seems the Australian government is pushing for answers on one of their citizens dying."

Elain unleashed a string of curses with many words I hadn't heard used in that context before.

"More inflection on the latter half, sweetie." Rhian gave a chuckle. "No one will take your cursing seriously if you drift off on emphasis halfway through the tirade."

"MI-5 and Neirin?" Elain let out an exasperated sigh. "You know how he is with authority."

"He said he'd be nice to them. I don't expect him back until tonight. MI-13 sent a counsellor with him to make sure MI-5 behaved. They like to use sunlight to threaten our kind. Your chief wants to make sure they didn't try that. What did you need?"

"I would have called Father, but you know he always leaves his phone in the crypt. Is he there?"

"No, sweetie. He and Rhodri are in conference. Mr Calhoun decided to have the race commission meeting early. Mayor Yardley barely arrived in time to scoot into the meeting before they locked the doors."

Another round of cursing erupted from Elain.

"Much better, dear. Now, what is the issue?"

"Yardley and his wife are top of the suspect list," Elain said. "Activate the alarms and lockdown. I'll come in through the lower garage. Are there any Bobbies on site?"

"No, they were dismissed when the inspector finished the investigation here."

"We will be there in ten minutes. Get the lockdown in place."

"Already done. Jonathan and I are beginning to search."

Elain clicked the phone off and goosed the accelerator.

"Hey, nice speed. Where are we going?" Jake said and phased into the back seat.

"Don't sit on my cat, dummy," I growled, risking a glance over my shoulder.

"Ick! Is there a ghost on me?" Punkin grumped. He wrapped his paws around the door handle to steady himself. "Better not be that creepy ex-boyfriend with his chickens."

Jake pulled a chicken out of the air and set it on Punkin's head. I laughed.

"Whatever he did, get it off me!"

I widened my eyes at Elain, trying not to laugh.

Elain did laugh, keeping her eyes glued to the twisting mountain road.

"Where are Bryce and Sir Reginald?" I risked another glance back at Jake. He was plucking feathers off his coat and casually laying them on Punkin. One turned real.

"It is that crazy boyfriend!" Punkin screeched. "I know there's something on me! Stop it, fool! I'll die and come hack hairballs on you!"

"Bryce and Reg are at the castle for the big meeting. They said one of them would come find you if anything happened."

"Get back there and tell them to keep an eye out for the

mayor or his wife. They could be trying to kill off Elain's father or the lieutenant colonel."

"Why would the mayor do that?"

"Jake! The mayor and his wife both are good at moving objects, like sharp pointy knives, with their magic. They could have gotten around the alarms on the weapons room by using magic to fling those knives at Bryce. That takes out one of the no votes against the mayor's big race."

"Oh! Okay." He plucked another feather off his jacket and started to tickle Punkin with it. This one turned normal too, and it brushed Punkin's ear before falling to the floor. Punkin screeched and hissed.

"Jake!"

"Going!" He phased out, then reappeared on the hood of Elain's car in the hood-ornament pose he had struck before. Fortunately, she couldn't see him, or her view of the road would have been lost. I laughed and told her what he had done.

"You have fun taste in boyfriends," she said.

The lower garage was a cave, hidden two-thirds of the way up the mountain. There was barely a dirt track through some scrub. Two trees looked about to end our mad run. She drove right through them as though they were ghosts like Jake.

"I know, a hidden cave. How cliché, right?" Elain steered us into the opening in the cliff face that hadn't been there a second before. The car's headlights lit a single creaky-looking old wood-and-iron elevator, barely large enough for her small sports car. It rose as soon as we stopped.

"Not going to call it the Raven Cave or something cool?"

"Lower garage is the best we've come up with. This used to be the escape tunnel from the stronghold. Father had to use it several times whenever the Normans got overly aggressive back in the twelfth and thirteenth centuries."

The lift creaked to a stop. Elain pulled her car forward and through a ghostly wall into the main garage we had left that morning. Pristine though dark marble walls surrounded us. Red and yellow lights lit the garage. Dim, but it was enough for us to see.

"Why is it so dark in here?" I had meant to ask earlier.

"We keep the caer darkened," Elain said. We tumbled out of the car and headed towards the elevator to the main level. "Mother, Father, and Neirin need little light because of their nature. I and most other fae barely need more than they do. You'll notice you see well in dim light."

Once in the elevator, she drew her wand.

"I need to tap both you and Punkin, so the alarm wards recognise you. Hold still." Her black wand glittered with purple waves of magic.

"Do I have super powers now?" Punkin asked.

"Super annoying isn't a super power," I said.

"I was hoping for venomous hairballs," he said. "Or a retractable tail dart thrower."

"No such luck," Elain said. "Your only power is being super annoying like normal."

The lift doors swooshed open, and the air before us, right at the doors, had a shimmer I hadn't noticed before.

"The waver is the lockdown field. It shouldn't harm you if I did the spell correctly."

"Super Pwca!" Punkin wailed and jumped through. No klaxons sounded. I followed Elain through into the grand hall. Elain had her phone out.

"Ebrel and I are in. We have Punkin as well."

"Jonathan is searching the upper levels," Rhian's voice sounded from the phone. Elain held it in front of her as we ascended the grand staircase. "I'm down in the crypts."

"Roger that," Elain said. "We'll take the second level. Is the commission meeting in the lounge next to the weapons hall?"

"Affirmative," Rhian said. "Out."

"Is it safe for your mother to search a level alone?" I was glad I had Elain and her hidden daggers with me. And smart-alec Punkin. I didn't want to face a killer who could levitate and through knives all by myself.

"Mother will be fine. She's a vamp, remember?"

"She'll drink their blood?"

"Super strong and super fast," Elain said. We made it to the weapons hall. "Stay to the side until I clear the room." She waved me away.

"This is where being able to fling tail darts would be useful," Punkin said.

Elain ignored him. Again her wand pulsed with the purple light. She tapped the double doors to the weapons hall, and they swung into the room.

"Stay here." She glanced at me. "Wand, silly girl. I hear you know how to blast demons. Do the same to anyone who tries to kill me."

"Oh. Right." I felt my cheeks warming. I reached into my sleeve and pulled it out.

A moment later, she was back.

"Clear. Neirin's flat is at the back side. The alarm spells on this side are intact."

"I should learn how to sense stuff like that," I whispered. "I feel like a kid on her first day of school."

"Bet you weren't searching for a killer on your first day in school."

"Nope. I was trying to stop Billy Tompkins from eating paste. Less exciting, but more useful right then."

"Let's check the back entrance to Neirin's flat. And my flat." She stopped at the ballroom doors. "Seals still intact," she said. "The ones the Bobbies put on, and our alarm spells."

"Wow!" Jake said, phasing in next to me. "You snuck in. I was watching the main drive."

"Elain's sneaky, Jake," I said. "Lady Sneak, remember?"

"I can't hear him, but the perp can hear you," Elain whispered.

We hurried towards the other door to Neirin's flat. Elain paused at one corner. She flattened against the wall and peered around the corner, holding her wand like a cop holding a handgun at the ready. She waved for me to follow.

At the door, she stepped to one side, motioning me to stay near the other. Again her wand flared with a cascade of violet energy.

"Nothing," she whispered. "Still intact. Let's check the loos on the way to my flat. Can your boyfriend check the gents'?"

"I'm on it!" Jake darted out in front of us, acting like a more pronounced version of the sneaky pose Elain just adopted. He clenched his hand hands together, with index fingers and thumbs straight out, like he was holding a gun.

Elain eased the door open. A moment later, she was back.

"Clear," Jake called, phasing through the door of the gents'.

"My flat next."

Jake raced ahead of us, floating a foot off the floor. Ghosts almost never had full legs. He could, if he wanted. When he moved, however, he only stayed visible down to his waist or knees.

Punkin charged in front of us, flicking his tail and making swooshing noises. "Tail darts, take that, baddie!"

Jake phased back through the closed door right as we stepped up to it.

"No one inside," he said. "You didn't rinse your coffee cups. You've got dried cream around the rims."

"Jake says no one's inside," I told Elain.

"He's handy for something," she said. Her wand pulsed again. "Lock spells still normal."

"You may have to get a spell to keep Jake out, though," I said. "His idea of personal space was always a tad sketchy."

"Keeping spirits out is tricky," Elain said and leaned back against the wall. "Rhosyn might be able to do it, I'm not sure. We might have to contract with a necromancer through MI-13 to get that type of spell. And necromancers are difficult to find. Dealing with the dead puts them on the fringes of good magic."

Elain tapped out a quick message on her phone.

We'll meet you in the study on the ground floor, Rhian's message flashed back.

"What's going on in the commission meeting?" Elain looked at me. I looked at Jake's ghost. He shrugged.

"The mayor was pleading his case," Jake said. "Both Bryce and Reg stayed to listen. I came out to wait on you two."

I passed that on.

"Three," Punkin said. "Everyone forgets about the familiar. If I had magic tail darts, no one would forget me."

"There's a reason you don't have them, Fuzzbum," Elain said. "Pardon my question, but does every ghost in the world know how to find you?"

I shrugged.

"Not every ghost," Jake said. "Once we cross over, we can find the people special to us. I can sense you no matter where you are."

"Oh, great," I said and relayed what he said. "So other ghosts like Sir Reginald can't just think about me and know where I am?"

"Maybe. I doubt it," Jake said. "If I think about my sister back in the States, I can figure out where to find her."

"She's your sister, so she's special. What about Sammi? Can you sense her?" She was the barista I trained to replace me right before I left for Britain. Jake shook his head. "Or what about Nia back at Mystic Brews?" Another shake.

"Interesting," Elain said and pushed herself off the wall. "Let's get to—" The phone in her hand vibrated and flashed red across the screen.

"To the ballroom!" She raced down the hall.

❧ 23 ❧

The door was ajar as I rounded the corner. Elain shouldered it open and rushed in. I was a step behind Punkin. Elain was in midair, diving at a figure reaching towards a table.

The old woman didn't stand a chance. Elain was on her, and they tumbled to the floor. Wind rushed out of the old woman's lungs. When they skidded to a stop by some of Sir Reginald's racing trophies, Elain had the woman's hands behind her back.

"Oh, I say," Sir Reginald said. "What is Seonag doing here?"

He and Bryce were in the room, along with Jake.

"Good show, my girl," the lieutenant colonel said.

"How's the meeting?" Elain asked and kneeled next to the woman, both of Seonag's arms twisted behind her back.

"Mostly done. The council denied a mixed race. We did support a fae-only race." The lieutenant colonel was searching through his inner coat pockets again. "I might have some cuffs in here. Let me look a bit."

"So you ducked out?" I asked.

"Had to use the loo," he said. "A-ha! Here you go, lass." He passed a pair of glowing green silver shackles to Elain. Once the cuffs were on, they pulled the woman to her feet.

"I be needin' ta find it," the woman whispered.

"Tell that wench to let her go," a voice hissed in the dark of the high ceiling above us. The door to the great ballroom slammed shut. A second later, pounding sounded on the door. Someone trying to get in.

The lieutenant colonel and Elain both fired red balls of light up. The orbs meandered above us, barely illuminating the vast empty chamber, still set as it had been for the wake.

"Elain," Rhian's muffled voice drifted through the door. "I can't enter. It's spell-locked."

"NOW! Tell them," Betrys Dewsberry said and drifted down from the recesses above.

"Mother! What? Why?" Sir Reginald said.

"Oh!" I breathed. My mind felt like a complicated clockwork, and a penny that had been jammed in the slot had finally dropped. The clockwork gears meshed now. "It all makes sense." I took a step back and bumped against another table. "Wow! I can't believe I didn't see it."

"Mother, please help us," Sir Reginald said.

My phone buzzed. A glance at my watch showed it was Aunt Rose.

I wasn't sure we could handle this by ourselves, so I grabbed one of my wireless earbuds out of my pocket. Once I had it in, I tapped my smartwatch.

"Betrys Dewsberry," I said, "why should Elain and the lieutenant colonel let Seonag go?"

Everyone turned to look at me.

"Because, my dear, I said so." She levelled her wand at me.

"Dearie," Aunt Rose said in my ear, "is Betrys there? Has she gone rogue?"

"It's not Betrys," I said, both to inform those trapped in here with me and to let Aunt Rose know. "Sir Reginald, that's not your mother. If the lieutenant—"

"Call me Rhodri, my dear," he said and backed his way towards me. His eyes darted around, not sure where the threat was. As he moved closer, his eyes dropped towards the glow on my wrist. I raised my hand to rub my cheek, confident he would see the words Call Active, Aunt Rose.

"Oh, good show," he whispered.

"Who is there?" Aunt Rose said through my earbud.

"If only Rhodri could see you, he or Elain would recognise you for what you are. What is your name, hag?"

"What?" Rhodri's hand jerked into his jacket, and he side-stepped away from me.

"A hag..." Aunt Rose's voice was cold. "One of those sea hags Rhodri goes on about?"

"You're one of Rhodri's sea hags... one he and Bernard Dewsberry didn't quite kill last time," I said.

"Very good, you little witch." The ghost floating above the ceiling shifted. The appearance of Betrys Dewsberry slid from her. Her form now glowed green. Hair of seaweed fluttered behind her as though she were underwater. Her loathsome old face and decrepit bent spectral body floated towards me. She wore a brownish-green dress, made of more flowing seaweed. "Tell them to let her go."

"What did you do to my mother?" Sir Reginald dived at the hag. She levelled her wand. A sick greenish light flared, and he tumbled back, head over misty heels.

"Listen, Ebrel," Aunt Rose said, "I'll help you get her visible to the others. They'll help hold her off until I can teleport to the caer. If she's as strong as I suspect, you need to buy us some time to break the spell locks she's set."

"What can I do?" I said to let Aunt Rose know I understood.

"Nothing, witchling," the hag said.

"Point your wand at her and repeat the words I say," said Aunt Rose. "There are going to be seven of them in Latin. Speed isn't important. Saying them exact is. She might even become somewhat corporeal. At least enough for the others to see and hear her."

"Tell your little girlie friend to remove the restraints," the hag snarled.

"She wants you to remove the cuffs," I told Elain.

"Fat chance! Is that the American phrase?"

The hag's wand flared. A bolt sizzled out of it. Elain could see the magic. She dodged, though not enough. The edge of the blast caught her. She and her prisoner tumbled to the floor again.

"Point your wand and repeat this phrase," Aunt Rose said. She pronounced each word. I whispered them. The hag's eyes darted to me at the next-to-last syllable, and she turned her wand on me. Mine was faster. The last sound cleared my mouth, and I pushed magic into the wand. A blast of greenish energy, bright and sparkling, zipped out and enveloped the hag's spirit.

"Blimey, it is her!" Rhodri said. He pulled a long black umbrella from inside his coat. "Where is that silly musket?"

Elain had a knife in the air, then another. They sailed right through the hag's ghost.

"Do as I say, or everyone in here, ghost and living, will feel my wrath!"

"You'll not kill us," Rhodri said. A half-eaten scone plopped to the floor. "Oh. Was saving that for a nosh later," he said and kept searching.

"What's going on, Ebrel?" Elain called. "Why can I hear her?"

"If they can hear me, I don't need you any longer, witch!" The hag's wand spit that sick sea-green light straight at me.

Punkin jumped in front and took the blast. He thudded into my chest, wheezing.

"She didn't..." He groaned and spasmed. "...set it for pwca. I'll recover. Hide."

"Where is my mother?" Sir Reginald called.

"Reg's mother is in cuffs," I yelled. Only the hag could be heard by Elain and Rhodri. I still had to translate for the other ghosts.

"What? The housekeeper?" Elain called. Her own wand spit purple fire that sparkled against the hag. It did little.

"Your living magic can't touch me. Now release the selkie."

"NO!" I called. "She needs the real Betrys to get the seal skin."

"Of course," Rhodri said. "Bernard was going to return it and set his wife free. You wanted the skin, though. He fought you, not her."

"Aye," Seonag called. She was hiding behind the tables, crouching low.

"Why does she need the housekeep... Sir Reginald's real mother to get the skin?" Elain asked, darting between tables. That earned another blast from the hag's bolt.

"To return to the living," Rhodri said. Another wand blast shattered the table in front of him. He crawled to another, then pulled a bunch of carrots out of his pocket. "Was going to give those to that family of wererabbits on the back side of the mountain. I forgot to visit them."

"Why does she need the skin to do that?" Elain called.

"They're both creatures of the sea," Rhodri said. A bear trap clanked to the floor as the hag fired another blast at him. More of Reg's trophies flew against the wall.

"Leave them alone!" Jake pulled a ghostly chicken from the air and flung it, overhand, at the sea hag's ghost. The chicken spiraled through the air like an American football and smacked the hag in the side of the head. She reeled back.

"You dare harm me, fool!"

Another ray from her wand splatted Jake's ghost through the back wall of the ballroom. Most of the feathers from his biker jacket fluttered and fell to the floor. A few of them turned solid. Another two dozen were still in ghostly form.

I remembered Elain taking the feather back in Barti Ddu's pub... Would it work? Could I? From where I crouched behind the wreckage of one of the blasted tables, this seemed like our only hope. Fortunately, Punkin crawled towards me.

"How do I make these solid?" I asked him.

"Make what solid?"

"There's a pile of ghost feathers here, from Jake."

"Um... I think I might have a concussion. You asked for solid ghost feathers?"

"Some familiar you are! Help me make these real."

"You're the boss, lady," he said. "Wand out, I'll guide. You owe me a bag of beans."

"If this works, you got it."

He put his paw on my wand. I sent a surge of my magic through the stick, and he tweaked the magic somehow. The feathers shifted and became real.

Elain crawled towards me. Bryce flew at the hag from behind and earned another blast from her wand. He dodged, expecting it. Reg dived in and knocked her sideways. Jake zipped back in through the wall and hovered near me.

"Here." I shoved the feathers towards Elain. "Make knives."

"Feathers?" Then she grinned. "Ghost-feather knives. To peg a ghost with!" She slid half a dozen feathers together and pulsed some magic into them. They blended and merged into a rough knife shape. She hefted it, testing the balance. "Not great, but throwable. I'll need more than this lot."

"Jake! I need a chicken!"

"Why?"

"Don't ask, just strip it and pile the feathers here, okay?"

"They're just ghost feathers," he said and pulled a ghost chicken out of the air. "The feathers won't hurt that hag."

"They will if I make them solid." I had an idea. I hoped it would work, and in time.

"You're weird," he said. "You know that, right?"

"I am not weird. Just do it!" I crawled away from Elain while she made more of the feather knives. A pile of feathers plopped in front of me. Jake sat behind a table. The chicken in his ghostly hands looked rather perturbed.

"Another. Don't argue, just do it, and don't call me weird again."

"He's right," Punkin said, "you are weird." He put his paw on my wand again. The feathers became solid. Thicker and stiffer than normal feathers. A few seconds later, we moved to the second pile of feathers.

"Can we do what Elain is doing?"

"Of course," Punkin said. "I'm skilled at transfigurations. Inanimate only. Otherwise I wouldn't still be a cat."

I made seven feather knives with his help. Above us, Reg and Bryce dodged and weaved at the hag.

"As fun as a good rugby scrum," Reginald called out, then caught a blast from the hag. He flew back through the wall.

"Here!" I slid the feather knives towards Elain.

"I need a distraction," Elain whispered.

I nodded, then looked at Punkin. The red light orbs still circling above gave his eyes an eerie gleam.

"Can you help me blast her?"

"I was wrong. You're not weird. You're crazy! But I like it. Carry me."

I scooped him up, his paw on my wand again. "Get her, Jake!"

"Why?"

"So I have a chance to stand. Go help Bryce."

He flew off. I peered across the top of the tables and stood when Jake dived into the spiritual melee. Bryce looked more haggard than the hag. I levelled my wand at her, Punkin's paw on my hand.

"Give me an opening," I called. Behind me, more rattles and thuds sounded as Rhodri kept searching his pockets. A wet splat of something gooey hit the floor.

"Wondered what I did with that pudding..."

"You think you're my match, witchling?" the hag called. I didn't wait and pushed magic into my wand, picturing the demon I had blasted. Punkin pushed a surge in, tweaking my magic. The blast hit the hag and slammed her semi-corporeal form back against the wall. Her return bolt at me went wide, striking the wall by the doors. They sizzled and crackled under the magical onslaught.

Elain charged forward. The first ghost-feather knife flew from her hands. It missed by a finger length and twanged into the wood of the wall. She plucked another from her belt and threw on the run. This one pegged the hag's gown under her right arm. The next one embedded through her gown under her left arm. Followed by another, then another. When she ran out of knives, the old sea hag was literally nailed to the wall by the knives made of spectral feathers. Her ghostly wand was aimed at a side wall, away from us.

"Here it is!" Rhodri called. "For Bernard, and all those you killed, vile hag!"

The blast of the musket set my ears ringing. I ducked and dropped Punkin. If anyone was shouting, I couldn't understand them. Echoes of the waves of the musket blast roared in my ears. The stench of brimstone clouded the air and clogged my nose.

When I got my eyes to focus again, I saw a red glow inside the green ghost of the sea hag. A swarm of little red dots zipped and zapped around throughout her form. She wailed and then sagged. Her spectral form shrank, stabilising at about half her original size.

The door crashed open. Aunt Rose led the charge with a dozen Bobbies and Inspector Jones behind her. Wand out, she sent a wave of pink energy at the hag. The Bobbies held open a sack sparking with magical energy. Aunt Rose plunged the ghost of the hag into the bag, and the Bobbie captain pulled the draw-string shut, sealing the spirit inside.

❧ 24 ❧

Aunt Rose said something. I shrugged and shook my head.

"I can't hear," I shouted. "Musket. Loud."

She tapped me with her wand, and my hearing settled down.

"That will fix you. Are you good, Ebrel?" Aunt Rose pulled me in for a hug. "No need for shouting. I'm mighty proud of you."

Beyond me, the Bobbies pulled Seonag along, right up to where Macsen and Rhian stood, their own wands out.

Sir Reginald floated right beside her, looking at her face.

Instead of an old woman, Seonag was young. With ageless beauty. Her eyes met mine.

"How did you figure me out?"

"I didn't," I said. "I finally realised Betrys wasn't really Bernard's wife."

"How?" Inspector Owain had one eyebrow cocked. "This one seems complicated."

"When we first interviewed Sir Reginald," I said.

"Please, my dear, call me Reg. We are friends by now, I hope."

"When Reg was at the café, and Betrys departed, she disturbed a cup."

"Of course," he said, a look of knowing on his face. "Ghosts rarely affect the physical world. Those who can are usually malicious spirits like poltergeists."

"Malicious is a good word for that hag," Rhodri said. He looked at Seonag. "Betrys wasn't your real name, was it?"

"No," Seonag said. The Bobbies removed the restraints from her. "Bernard and I agreed that I'd take another name to hide my family. Seonag is my birth name. When the hag found us on that day in Swansea, she captured me and took my appearance. She locked me in the form of an old crone."

"And used a spell to keep you from telling of her?"

"Aye," Seonag said. "I was on my way to meet Bernard and get my seal skin back. Our marriage was over, and he lived up to his word. But the hag intervened before he could reveal where he had hidden it. The sea hag took my place. I can only guess that Bernard sensed her ruse. That was why the battle was so fierce. Me heart broke seeing all the dead and injured caused because of me."

"Not because of you," I said. "The hag needed your skin. With it, she would make herself whole again."

"We didn't kill her dead enough, then." Rhodri sighed. "I was afraid one of them might have escaped." He patted his musket. "These depleted demonic rounds are good but unreliable. Never sure just how much energy the little buggers still have."

"Can you help her?" Reg asked. "I want my mother to be whole again. After all these years, she deserves it."

"Go ahead, lass," Rhodri said, once I relayed Reg's request. "Your eyes tell me you know what none of the rest of us do."

"The spell the hag put you under," I said to Seonag, "it kept you from sensing your skin?"

"Aye. Only these last few years had her spell faded enough for me to get a general location. It be here. Somewhere. But I cannae sense enough to know where. That's why I kept sneaking in. With her spell on me, I was not able to say why I was here, nor who I was."

The table with Reg's cricket equipment was overturned. Trophies, shoes, bats all lay scattered about.

"Bernard," I said. "was good at transformations, correct?"

"That he was, lass," Rhodri said. "He'd have made it look so mundane, she wouldn't know it, and he'd lock away its ability to call to her. That should have faded with his death, though."

"Except the sea hag blocked her ability to sense it. Somehow the hag recovered from what that first explosion did to her. She wasn't dead, though her sister hags were. So she went after Bernard. But she outsmarted herself and blocked Seonag's ability to sense where the skin was. Even in her ghost form, the now-dead sea hag couldn't find the skin. Without it, she'd stay in ghost form."

"With the damage of that battle in Swansea, I'm surprised the hag could reform," Rhodri said. "Bernard must have given her as good as he got. He wasn't one to back off a fight, not against a hag. There's a lot of evil in her if she can survive their fight and come back as a malicious spirit capable of casting spells from the afterlife."

"The hag... whom I believed was my mother," Sir Reginald added, his tone one of exasperation. "She only found me a few weeks ago. But she had to have been active a year ago to cause my demise. What was she doing all those years between my father's death and now?"

"Probably reforming her spirit," Aunt Rose said. "Just like Rhodri's favourite rakshasa demon is doing."

"He's going to be rather bothersome when he does return," the colonel added.

Something still bothered me.

"The hag's... geas—is that the compulsion spell?" Everyone nodded. I'd used the correct term. "Her geas on Seonag was still active. Once the hag's spirit recovered from the Swansea battle and found that Reginald's mother was in Reg's home, still disguised, she hatched a new plan. She wanted to use Seonag as the gateway back to the mortal world. But Seonag would need to get her seal skin back," I said, staring down at the remains of the table and all it held. "The hag planned to use the magic of the seal skin's transformation to invade your body and make it her own. She'd get her life back by sacrificing yours."

"Bravo!" Rhian said. "You have a good grasp of magic for someone so new to this."

"I watch too many mystery shows," I confessed. "I love the old mysteries. Especially the BBC ones."

"Please," Reg said. "Help my mother be whole again."

I reached down and pulled at the old equipment bag. It was faded and stained.

"The initials in the corner are not RD, are they?"

Reg shook his head.

"That was Father's bag. The bottom of the B for Bernard has faded."

I passed the bag to Seonag. As her fingers clenched it, the old canvas shifted and became dark brown. She flipped it around her shoulders and shimmered into the form of a seal. Another shimmer, and she was human again.

"My dear," Rhodri said, "this old man would like to make amends. If I may, I would like to escort you back to the shores where your family swims and apologise to them for my part in this fiasco."

"Oh, Rhodri." She hugged him and kissed his whiskered

cheeks. "I accept. Your apologies and your offer. You are a dear friend. Ye made me proud as his foster father."

"So," Inspector Owain interrupted, "I think I see how Sir Reginald died. The hag needed him out of the way. He'd left the equipment bag with Rhodri, and she needed it. But she wasn't sure which item was the skin. And her spell on Seonag was still in operation. The hag had to wait for it to wear off. That took decades."

"Aye," Seonag said. "Part of the geas I was under was to avoid Rhodri. Otherwise he might have realised the hag's deception. That's why I was never around him when he came to visit Reginald. And I was unable to enter his home, where Sir Reginald left his cricket equipment."

"I was closer to the stadium," Rhodri said. "He'd come spend the day before a match with me, and then return after. Always left his kit there, knowing I'd keep it safe."

"So the sea hag used her spells to poison Reg on his last drive. His cricket gear would come out for the memorial service. Seonag could find the skin, and the hag could take a bridge back from death. However, she committed too perfect of a crime," Owain said. "We were unable find Reginald's car without Ebrel's assistance.

"Quite the lucky break that I ran into your young man," Reg said. "He said you'd be able to hear me and help rectify the situation."

Jake pulled himself more upright. A large smile played across his face.

"I wouldn't have figured this out without my friends," I said. "Jake helped connect me to Reginald. Owain and Aunt Rose taught me how to handle a demon—kind of. I don't want to do that again. Ever."

"I suspect the sea hag bored holes in the engine cauldron of the car," Owain said. "Never heard of a ghost reaching into the physical world other than a few times they were attached to an object."

"A hag would have centuries of experience," Aunt Rose added. "More than enough power to affect spells like the cauldron's protection. Though she might have to spend more time doing so than we would. To move a physical object would take even more time. Magic bridges the material and spiritual worlds, so she'd be more able to affect the cauldron's spells than move the bag."

"A demon escape would alert us to Reginald's wreck," Owain said. "And cover her magic poisoning of his mind. Lucky we were there when the thing escaped. And the timing worked out well for the hag. The racing commission was in town; she could cast the blame on both Bryce and Yardley."

"And the hag could use her spells in the real world to move objects, like knives," Elain said.

"Aye," Seonag added. "Bryce Rustle came across me in the ballroom last night. Something smacked into his back. He gasped and fell dead. I smelled seaweed and figured it was the hag's ghost again. I ran, afraid you'd blame me for that death too."

"So Yerdleh is cleared of both murders," Owain said.

"Wait," Bryce asked, "where is Yerd-bum?"

I shrugged and passed that on.

"We ran out of the commission meeting so fast," Macsen said, "I didn't pay attention. Jonathan escorted the humans down to the study to offer refreshments and keep them out of harm's way."

Bryce disappeared through the wall. He returned a moment later.

"Found him," Bryce said. "He's got himself a nice pixie gal. They're having a bit o' fun down in the garage."

"R is for Rachel," I said and looked at Elain.

"Both the Yardleys have a pixie liaison," she said. "I wonder which started first?"

"That be none of our business, dearie," Aunt Rose said. "They must work that out amongst themselves."

The Robert who was captain of the Bobbies returned.

"Got the perp stowed in our high-security transport," he said. "Will you accompany it to MI-13 Spectral Detention?"

"If you will all excuse me," Owain said. "The paperwork on this one will take me at least a week to fill out."

"I'm wrung out," I said and leaned back against one of the few tables not decimated by the magical duel. "Any chance your Jonathan could make me a caramel macchiato? I need one like the pixies do."

"My dear Ebrel," Lady Edeirnion said, "you are welcome at Castle Raven for a caramel macchiato any time. Welcome to Misty Valley."

25

A week later, I cursed as I banged my knee on one of the antique tables Aunt Rose had stored in the small bedroom above the café. Punkin raised his head.

"Shhh. Cat nap in progress."

"Get your bum out of bed," I growled. "I just heard a truck pull in. My roaster is here."

"You've grouched about it all morning," he said, stretching. "I better go see what the fuss is about."

"You should know, after you tried those green coffee beans."

"Blech! Those are not coffee beans."

"Yes, they are. We have to roast them and bring out the flavours," I said.

Downstairs, Red was already in the kitchen. He and the delivery man hefted boxes down into the cellar. I followed them down. The magic lights flicked on as they progressed.

"Funny, I didn't figure those were magic the first day."

"No, but you squished me behind the coffee bags," Punkin said. "Can't ever snack in peace around here."

"I'll get yer machine put together," Red said and patted me

on the shoulder. "But only if you keep Punkin out of my way. Deal?"

"Okay, we'll both get out of your way," I said. "I just want to see it."

Red opened the box. Stainless steel glinted back at me. That looked like the roasting drum.

"I already had the gas line installed," Red said. "And the vents. Now, if it all lines up, I'll have it installed by tonight. If you get the furball out o' me way."

"Going. Come on, Fuzzbutt."

"You're sure those underripe nasty green pellets are really coffee?"

"Yep. Roasting is an art form. I'm not great at it, but I will get better."

Elain met me in the kitchen.

"Brought you a present," she said. A dinner-plate-sized package wrapped in bright paper was under her arm. "Let's get out of their way."

We headed into the café. It was dim, with the blinds drawn. Nia and Mia were prepping for the tea crowd. Today was the first day I'd be able to provide espresso bar service at the same time. Nia had progressed, but not enough to handle the shift on her own.

Atop my espresso machine sat the carved wooden dragon I had seen down at the Art Emporium. Io had brought it to me as a belated birthday present. I touched it as I walked by. That was my new little gesture, sure it would bring me some luck. Or at least connect me to my family.

Aunt Rose, with her apron on, brought out two plates, each with a warm scone covered in clotted cream. Nia set two mugs in front of us.

"I'm practicing." She waved at the espresso machine. "See how these taste."

"Caramel macchiato?" Elain asked.

"If I make them"—Nia grinned—"they're caramel tornados. Someday I'll make them as good as Ebrel's."

I sipped.

"Very good. Tomorrow, we'll test you. Let you make a mocha."

"Your present," Elain said and pushed the gift towards me, then scooped a bite of scone onto her fork.

"You didn't need to..."

"I kind of missed your birthday," she said. "And since you're my... BFD now..."

"You mean BFF? Best Friend Forever?"

"Exactly. Now open it."

I did and whistled.

"A leprechaun teleportation disc?"

"It's keyed to a matching one at my flat," she said. "I didn't want to blow my trust fund to get one of their unlimited destination discs. Those are pricy. I'm surprised Gemma de Yardley could afford one."

She slid a silver bracelet across the table. "This is the second part. I already asked Rhosyn."

"Asked her what?"

"If she minded you being my roommate at the caer." Elain grinned. "Mother enchanted the bracelet herself, keyed to you. You wear it and don't get caught in most of the security magic."

"Most of?"

"Mum and Dad's personal space is off limits, as is Neirin's flat. Mother and Father can go anywhere. They and Neirin need to escort us into their inner crypts. Yours is like mine, except for a few rooms, like the weapons hall. But you shouldn't go in there alone anyway. Too many traps about."

"Seriously? You want a roomie?" Something fuzzy rubbed against my legs.

"Say yes, silly girl," Punkin said. "I want more room than that decrepit old bed you sleep on.

"Umm... he's right," I said. "I'm stuck with him."

"Already considered," Elain said. "But Mother insists he wear a security collar while there. If not, she'll leave him stuck in any magic traps he tries to break through."

"Not a problem," Punkin said.

"If you go where you shouldn't," Elain said, tilted sideways to look at Punkin under the table, "I'll let Neirin be the one to educate you about etiquette."

"You wouldn't! Not him." Punkin shivered, rocking against my leg.

"You bet your fuzzbum I would. Mother will too. Neirin is already sharpening his knives for the time. He says he wonders what you'd look like without fur."

"Um... I'm going to go pack..." He ran up the stairs.

Elain laughed.

"I so look forward to that day," Elain said. "We all know he'll try to sneak past a ward."

"Seriously? Your roomie? This is so weird."

Elain raised her cup and sipped. "Very good, Nia."

The pixie smiled her thanks and kept working.

"It's not weird," Elain said. "You're my friend. I get lonely at the caer. Mother and Father like you. Even Neirin said he'd be nice to you and lay off his smitten-fool routine. At least for the first day you're with us."

"And the teleport pad is for getting back and forth?"

"Of course. We've wanted a way to pop into the village when we needed anyway. Rhosyn was nice enough to agree, as long as it's only my family and you." She glanced at Nia and Mia. "Sorry, staff members still have to go by normal means."

"No worries," Mia called. "Pixies rarely teleport. We like to stretch our wings, unlike you tall fae."

"So, will you take my spare room?" Elain asked. "I've not had a roomie before, except at MI-13's academy, and I was far too busy there to pay any attention to what she was doing."

"You know the ghosts always seem to find me," I said. "We'll have more adventures like last week."

"Mother said as long as the adventures don't wreck her ballroom, she's happy to have you." Elain grinned and scooped more scone and cream onto her fork.

"What do you want for rent?"

"How about you make macchiatos or lattes each evening," she said. "Even pixie magic isn't as good as yours. You've got the touch."

"You sure you're happy with this? I mean ghosts, Punkin, and you..." I grinned, understanding. "And you'll get to see more of Io. We've got another wanding lesson this evening."

"I was hoping for that," she said. A sly grin showed from behind her mug.

"Ghosts and fae," I said and shook my head. "I didn't think that would be my life in Wales."

"Lattes and spirits," Elain added. "It's what you're best at."

The End

Ebrel's adventures will continue. You can preorder the next story, *Tall, Dark and Troll* on Amazon!

MORE MISTY VALLEY

Don't worry!

More of Misty Valley is on the way. Book 2, *Tall, Dark and Troll* is scheduled for release on March 28, 2020.

Thanks, or Diolch, as they say in Wales, for reading *Lattes and Spirits*, Book One of the Welsh Witch series.

If you haven't already, you can sign up for my email newsletters. Emails are delivered by interwebz pixies about every two weeks. More often around book launches.

Please, if you enjoyed this story, would you head over to Amazon, Bookbub and/or Goodreads to leave a review. For authors, reviews are like Carmel Tornados are to pixies. They not only keep us writing, but they also help us land promotional deals and attract the attention of media.

Diolch o Galon!

- Alyn Troy

Printed in Great Britain
by Amazon